The Lady He Loathed

ROGUES OF MULL
BOOK THREE

Jayne Castel

All characters and situations in this publication are fictitious, and any resemblance to living persons is purely coincidental.

The Lady He Loathed, by Jayne Castel

Published by Winter Mist Press

ISBN: 978-1-991280-06-0 (Paperback)

Edited by Tim Burton
Cover design by Winter Mist Press
Cover images generated by Midjourney and courtesy of Depositphotos.com

Visit Jayne's website: www.jaynecastel.com

No matter how much they hated each other ... fate tied them together. Two sworn enemies are shipwrecked—and are forced to confront the dark secret they both share. Scars, sacrifices, and high adventure in Medieval Scotland.

Years ago, Astrid Maclean's best friend died in a tragic accident ... but Astrid doesn't believe it *was* an accident. Instead, she holds one man responsible.

Finn MacDonald carries a heavy burden, one that he shares with no one. After a decade away at war, he now serves the Macleans of Duart on the Isle of Mull. However, he still holds a deep resentment toward the locals who once tried to hang him—and the woman who incited their hatred.

When the clan-chief charges them both with a vital mission on the eve of war with the neighboring clan, Astrid and Finn are forced to work alongside each other.

They set off to get help from allies, but when a violent storm hits their ship and they are shipwrecked on a desolate isle, their journey goes awry.

Suddenly, two sworn enemies are thrown together in a fight for survival.

And when they are, the truth about the past ... and how they really feel about each other ... is finally revealed.

THE LADY HE LOATHED is Book Three of an exciting new trilogy by Jayne Castel—full of flawed yet irresistible Highland warriors and determined Scottish lasses!

*"If you were born with the weakness to fall,
you were born with the strength to rise."*
—Rupi Kaur

1: FORGIVE OR FORGET

Duart Castle
Isle of Mull, Scotland

May 1315

THE HORSE CLATTERED into the outer courtyard, foam flying from its mouth.

Descending from the walls, Finn MacDonald's gaze narrowed. He'd seen the horse from a distance, racing along the clifftops from the north, its rider crouched low over the saddle.

They were traveling with urgency, and Finn had called out to the guards below to open the gates and winch up the portcullis.

Whoever the rider was—he had news. And judging from the grim lines of the man's sweat-slicked face, as he swung down from the saddle, it wasn't good.

"I bring word from Dounarwyse," the warrior greeted Finn without preamble. He was breathing hard, his blue eyes wide. "We've spied a fleet of birlinns heading down the coast toward the broch." His throat bobbed. "They're flying the Mackinnon banner."

Finn's mouth thinned. "Of course, they are." That came as no surprise. Kendric Mackinnon had been sharpening his dirk for months now, biding his time. However, this man's mention of a 'fleet' of ships did take him aback. As far as Finn knew, Mackinnon's alliance with the MacDonalds of Sleat on Skye had fallen through—their enemy didn't have such resources.

"How many galleys?" he asked then.

"We counted twenty."

Finn's gut clenched. *Twenty?* How the devil had 'The Butcher of Dùn Ara' managed to amass such a force?

"Our scouts on the coast spied MacNab and MacGregor banners flying on some of the masts," the warrior gasped, answering his unvoiced question while he struggled to recover his breath. "The Mackinnons have found new allies."

Finn breathed a curse, even as a chill rippled down his spine. This was the last thing they needed. The Macleans of Duart had only five birlinns at their immediate disposal, and it would take a day or two for help to come from Moy, Croggan, and Breachacha once word went out.

He gestured to a stable lad to take the messenger's horse before nodding toward the keep that rose above them. "Come on," he said curtly, masking his worry with a brusque manner that had served him well over the years. "The clan-chief needs to hear this."

Loch Maclean's face hardened as the messenger relayed the news to him. "That treacherous bastard," the laird growled. "I wondered what he was up to."

Standing by the window, Finn nodded. "Aye, it's been nearly three months since MacKinnon's hopes for an alliance with the MacDonalds of Sleat turned to smoke ... but he's clearly been busy in the meantime."

Across the solar, the laird's sister gave a soft snort. *"Clearly."*

Finn frowned. Astrid Maclean rarely addressed him directly, yet he could always rely on her to make a jibe at his expense. Her tone now intimated that he'd just stated the obvious. Heat ignited under his ribs as he marked the glint in her peat-brown eyes.

Aye, the lady rarely missed the opportunity to make her disdain for him clear.

And likewise, he paid her the same compliment. The mere sight of the woman made his hackles rise. She was a constant reminder of a past he wished he could bury. There were still plenty of folk locally who looked at him askance, but while he found most of them easy to ignore, he loathed Astrid Maclean with a force that made his gut cramp.

Only, now wasn't the time to lob an equally sharp comment back at her. Not in the face of such dire news.

"How in Hades did he manage to secure the help of the MacNabs and the MacGregors?" Loch went on.

"They're Mackinnon allies," Astrid pointed out, "although from what I've heard, they have more to do with the Mackinnons of Strathardle ... than those of Mull."

"Kendric Mackinnon is out for more than blood now," Mairi, Loch's wife, spoke up then. She sat opposite Astrid, by the hearth, her tawny eyes wide, her face taut. "Tara's disappearance has likely twisted him ... turned his loathing for the Macleans into something far more dangerous. I wouldn't be surprised if he emptied his coffers or offered up his son in marriage to one of his new allies to achieve his end."

Silence followed these ominous words, and Finn's breathing grew shallow. "He doesn't know where Tara is, does he?" he asked, as a suspicion caught hold in his mind.

Loch's mouth pursed. "Let's hope he doesn't ... or he won't just *lay siege* to Dounarwyse ... he'll pull the broch apart stone by stone before he disembowels my cousin."

Finn pulled a face before muttering, "He'll do that anyway."

Back in March, the laird's cousin, Jack, had abducted Mackinnon's daughter, in a bid to take revenge on him. Years earlier, Kendric Mackinnon had murdered his father, and Jack had never been able to let his rage go. However, the abduction hadn't gone quite as planned, and Jack had lost his heart to the flame-haired beauty. Tara had returned home to her kin, only to run away hours later to be with Jack—and they'd lived at Dounarwyse in the months since.

To their knowledge, the Mackinnon clan-chief had no idea where his daughter had gone, yet he was no fool.

Perhaps it had dawned on him that she'd fallen in love with her captor. Even so, Mackinnon wouldn't know where Jack was. Until recently, he'd lived here at Duart Castle. Now, he captained his brother's guard at Dounarwyse. A large defense of eighty warriors guarded the castle—however, against the fleet of twenty birlinns that sailed toward them, it wouldn't be enough.

Drawing in a sharp breath, Loch focused on the messenger once more. "I'll give ye a fresh horse, but I need ye to return swiftly Dounarwyse," he instructed. "Tell the laird that help is on its way ... and that he must hold the castle until it arrives."

"Aye, Maclean," the warrior replied, although his expression was grim.

"Get yerself some food and drink from the kitchens first," Loch added, perhaps taking note of the man's exhaustion.

"Thank ye." With that, the messenger nodded, turned on his heel, and left the solar, the door thudding shut behind him.

Finn stepped away from the window. He was naturally impatient, not one to ever sit still for long, yet the need to act now boiled inside him. "Shall I ride for Croggan Tower and Moy Castle and tell Logan and Leod to rally their warriors?"

To his surprise, Loch shook his head. "Send one of yer men to do that ... and others across to Breachacha. My chieftains have all assured me of their loyalty ... let's test it." Loch paused then, raking a hand through his long dark hair. His gaze focused on Finn, narrowing slightly. "But if Mackinnon has roped in other clans, our own resources won't be enough."

"Ye must call upon the Macleods of Skye, brother," Astrid announced, rising gracefully from her chair, and pushing her long pale-gold hair from her shoulders. "They owe us a debt."

Loch glanced his sister's way. "Aye ... since we've reestablished ties with them, it's time to see if Tormod Macleod will remember our old alliance."

Finn's lips compressed at these words. Indeed, Loch had been in close contact with the Macleod clan-chief over the past months, but Tormod hadn't made him any promises.

"We must work quickly," Astrid said as she moved toward her brother. The lady's chin rose, her dark eyes filled with determination. "I shall go to Skye and relay yer call to arms in person."

Loch's mouth curved into a thin smile. "Aye, Astrid ... if anyone can convince auld Tormod Macleod to help us, it's ye."

Finn fought a sneer. Once, Loch had locked horns with his headstrong sister, yet these days, he appreciated her strategic mind and quick thinking. They worked closely together. Too closely for Finn's liking, for it meant that, as Captain of the Duart Guard, he saw far too much of the harpy.

And whenever their paths crossed, their scorn for each other was blistering. Astrid still looked at him as if he was a murderer, and he still recalled how she'd bayed for his blood over a decade earlier. Neither of them was prepared to forgive ... to forget. Indeed, their hatred for each other had deepened over the years.

All the same, there was a part of him—a tiny part—that grudgingly admired her cleverness.

Loch shifted his attention from Astrid then, focusing upon Finn instead. "My sister will be departing for Skye at first light tomorrow." Loch's dark eyes glinted, and Finn tensed. He knew that look well. His friend was up to something. "And *ye* shall escort her."

2: TOO DEEP A SCAR

ASTRID TENSED, HEAT igniting in her belly. She then cut her brother a sharp look. "MacDonald is needed here, Loch," she replied, her voice sharpening. "Send someone else with me to Skye."

MacDonald. Even referring to the whoreson by his clan-name choked her.

She had to focus on getting to Skye as swiftly as possible, and on gaining their allies' assistance. It was bad enough she had to suffer Finn's presence daily, for, as Captain of the Duart Guard, he worked closely with the laird. But the thought of traveling with him pushed her over the edge.

His sneering company was the last thing she needed on such an important mission.

This was her chance to prove herself to her brother—to herself—and she didn't want anything, or *anyone,* jeopardizing it.

The previous autumn, Loch had tried to force a marriage upon her, brokering an alliance with the Mackinnons of Dùn Ara and promising her to the clan-chief. Astrid had fought Loch and even tried to run away, but he'd refused to relent. Eventually, it had all gotten too much, and to her infinite shame, she'd sickened.

Even now, her pulse quickened, and her palms turned clammy, at the memory of the despair that had swallowed her, the darkness that had closed in.

Was that how she reacted in a crisis? She merely crumbled?

No, she had to find a way to drive this *weakness* out of her.

In the end, after finally reading the missive their father had left him, and after realizing his sister would die if he pressed things, Loch relented—severing the promise he'd made Kendric Mackinnon and making an enemy of him. In the months that followed, brother and sister had slowly rebuilt the shattered trust between them. Nevertheless, Loch had a bullish streak. When he set his mind on something, he wouldn't be moved.

Loch's gaze narrowed now. She didn't usually speak to him in such an acerbic fashion—not these days—but Astrid hadn't been able to contain herself. He knew she loathed the Captain of the Duart Guard, and yet he was about to force his company on her.

"I *can* spare him," he replied. "I've just hired a new marshal ... and I shall also manage the Guard myself while Finn is away." Her brother paused then, his gaze fusing with hers. "I want to ensure yer safety on the trip, Astrid ... and Finn's the only man I'd trust with yer care."

Heat washed over Astrid at these words, and it took all her self-control not to snort a bitter laugh. Unfortunately, her brother was close to Finn—and was blind to his flaws.

Her gut clenched then. The fact remained that Finn MacDonald had gotten away with *murder*. He'd taken her best friend, Maggie Garvie, away from her.

"Yer sister is right, Loch ... choose someone else for this mission," Finn spoke up then. As often, his tone was off-hand, dismissive. "We won't work well together ... ye know that."

Astrid started at this statement. Her enemy had spoken the truth, although he didn't usually acknowledge the hostility that boiled between them.

Silence fell in the solar. Meanwhile, Mairi's gaze flicked nervously between Loch, Astrid, and Finn's faces, her eyes shadowed now.

Astrid was aware the tension that filled a room whenever she and Finn occupied it at the same time must be tiring. All the same, she couldn't help it.

The man was a murderous snake. His very presence here was an offense to Maggie's memory.

Loch eventually shattered the silence, his curse reverberating off the stone walls.

Astrid flinched. Her brother usually kept his temper, yet his peat-dark eyes—the same shade as her own—were narrowed now as he stared Finn down. "Enough," he growled. "This nonsense has gone on for too long."

Astrid's already fast pulse jolted. "*Nonsense?*" she gasped.

Loch's attention cut to his sister. "Eleven years ago, a tragedy rocked our community when Maggie drowned," he ground out. "And aye, it was fresh and raw then, and ye had every right to vent yer spleen. But those days are long gone, and the tension between ye and Finn affects everyone here."

Anger washed over Astrid in a blistering wave. Her brother made her sound unreasonable. "Time doesn't matter," she countered. "Some wrongs leave too deep a scar."

Astrid deliberately didn't look Finn's way as she spoke, despite that she could feel his stare boring into her. She could taste his scorn.

"That's right," Finn murmured then. "They do."

Astrid stiffened, her heart racing now. She didn't like the intimation in his voice, as if *she* had wronged *him*. Aye, she'd incited the locals at Craignure into violence after Maggie's death—but someone had to do something. She hated that Finn acted like the injured party. He wasn't the victim of injustice, Maggie was. It galled her that he'd never paid for his crime.

However, Loch's expression was now intractable.

A pit opened in Astrid's belly when she realized her brother wasn't going to relent.

"I don't deny the dislike ye two have for each other." His voice hardened then. "But there is no place for it here. War casts its shadow over us all ... in the weeks to come, everything might change for the Macleans. We need to stop fighting amongst ourselves and focus on the Mackinnons." He stepped forward, his gaze sweeping from his sister to his friend. "End it now ... for I won't tolerate ye at each other's throats any longer."

"Curse ye, Loch!" Astrid let the knife fly from her hand, watching as it embedded in the cloth-covered round of wood on the far wall of her bedchamber. "Ye could have sent anyone with me ... just not *him!*"

Lord, she'd come close to losing her temper in the solar earlier. A red veil had dropped over her eyes when Loch made it clear he wouldn't discuss the matter any longer.

Finn had looked as incensed as her. His lean face was pale and taut, his mouth thin, as he'd turned on his heel and stalked from the solar. The captain couldn't linger in their presence anyway, for he had plenty to organize before their departure. At dawn, they'd be setting off in one of the clan-chief's birlinns, the *Sea Eagle*, on a journey that would take them two full days.

Breathing hard, Astrid whipped out a second knife from the belt she wore around her hips. Shortly, her maid, Gordana, would come up and they would pack a couple of bags with essentials for the trip. But for the moment, Astrid had some time alone—and the first thing she'd done was draw out her dirk and belt of throwing knives before laying them reverently on the bed.

She wouldn't be going anywhere without her weapons.

Astrid glanced over at the dirk lying atop the coverlet, its long thin blade encased in a leather scabbard. Her father's marshal had given her a knife-wielding lesson on her sixteenth birthday, and soon afterward, the laird himself had agreed to have a dirk and throwing knives made especially for his strong-willed daughter.

Astrid's lips thinned then. Loch didn't like her bearing weapons. However, it made sense for her to have something to defend herself with when traveling. Her brother wouldn't approve of her practicing with her throwing knives either—but what Loch didn't know wouldn't hurt him.

She'd worked hard to excel at knife-throwing over the years Loch had been away at war, and she was loath to lose her skills.

Jaw clenching, Astrid looked away from her dirk and sighted the target.

It was difficult though, for when she raised her hand, she noticed it was shaking.

Curse it, she hated how sensitive she was—how easily life knocked her around. Sometimes it felt as if she were clinging on by her fingertips.

She was all churned up inside now, a storm of emotions battling each other. Outrage and upset that her wishes had been ignored. Anxiety at the news that Kendric Mackinnon was bearing down upon Dounarwyse Castle with a fleet of birlinns—he'd have arrived at his destination by now—and guilt that she was focused on her hate for Finn while the enemy was breathing down their necks.

Astrid drew in a slow, deep breath, in an attempt to calm herself.

Satan's cods, how was she going to weather his company?

"It'll only be a few days. Ye don't have to talk to the bastard," she ground out, her grip tightening on her knife hilt. Her gut twisted then at her brother's insistence that the pair of them end their feud.

She couldn't put the past aside—not after what Finn had done—but she'd have to be quieter about her loathing for him in the future. Her brother had made it clear that he wouldn't tolerate either of them bringing their personal grievances into his home any longer.

It galled her to swallow her rage, yet she'd heed him.

Deep down, she understood why Loch had taken such a firm stance. It wasn't fair on Mairi either, the way she and Finn snarled and glowered at each other. And it had gotten worse of late, as if the resentment between them were a pot of boiling milk, about to spill over.

Muttering another curse under her breath, Astrid tried to focus on practicing with her knives.

Lining herself up as Donald, the old marshal, had shown her, she positioned herself with one leg before the other, her weight on the opposite leg to her throwing arm. Sighting the target once more, she breathed slowly, waiting until her hand steadied. Then, she brought the blade back behind her shoulder and swung it in an arc, releasing the blade halfway. The small narrow blade flew from her hand, spinning through the air before it thudded into the center of the target.

A thin smile compressed Astrid's mouth as she imagined the knife had just embedded itself to the hilt in Finn MacDonald's chest.

3: HOW WILL I SUFFER HIM?

"ARE YE SURE ye are happy to embark on this mission, Astrid?" Mairi asked, lowering the arrowhead she held. She was about to insert it into the split end of a yew shaft.

Astrid glanced up from where she'd been winding a thin coil of rope around her own arrow, securing the iron point in place, before grimacing. "I'm happy enough about the mission itself," she replied. "Just not the company."

"Ye aren't nervous about meeting with the Macleods then?"

"A little," Astrid admitted. "Who knows how difficult Tormod Macleod will be?" She paused then, her mouth quirking. "However, negotiating is what I do best. I enjoy pitting my wits against others ... and I'm pleased Loch is putting his trust in me."

Finishing securing the arrowhead, she made a quick knot and then placed the shaft in the long basket at her feet, where a pile of completed arrows was steadily growing. It was her and Mairi's habit, in the late afternoon before supper, to do a little 'women's work'— yet, today, there was a huge batch of arrows that had to be made.

"I'm in awe of ye," Mairi replied then, a smile flowering across her face. "Ye know that?"

Astrid inclined her head. "Really?"

"Aye."

"Why?"

"I like that ye are a woman who constantly forgets her place."

Astrid laughed at that, the sound traveling through the women's solar, where the two ladies sat. "I'm not sure my brother enjoys that aspect of my character," she admitted, shaking her head.

Mairi's dark-gold eyes twinkled. "Aye, he does ... Loch needs strong women in his life, or his arrogance would get out of hand."

Astrid snorted another laugh, even as her chest constricted.

She wanted to think of herself as being 'strong'—like Mairi was. However, recent events had made her doubt herself. Aye, she could be feisty and opinionated at times, but that wasn't what truly mattered. It was how a person dealt with a crisis that showed their true mettle.

And Mairi had shown hers. She'd weathered much in her life, including a broken heart when Loch had departed for war. Then, after her father died, she'd taken over the running of his inn. She was kind and big-hearted. However, as Loch had discovered, Mairi wasn't to be underestimated. Under her gentle façade was strength, resilience, and a will of iron. As such, she'd stepped into her new life was ease.

The two women fell into a companionable silence then, each focusing on their task. Meanwhile, the clang of metal from the weaponsmith in the outer courtyard drifting in through the small window was a constant reminder of what was coming.

Astrid's mood sobered as she worked. The castle had been in turmoil all day, following the news of the Mackinnon fleet bearing down on Dounarwyse. Loch had already sent scouts north to report on what was happening at the broch, while he readied his men to join the Macleans of Dounarwyse the following morning.

Everything was changing. It felt as if she were standing on shifting sand. Queasiness rose then, making her belly churn as she thought of the violence to come. For years, her father had indulged in skirmishes with his northern neighbors, yet things were different now.

This was no skirmish but a reckoning between their clans— one that would decide everything.

Eventually, when Astrid had completed another five arrows, she set aside her work and rose to her feet. Stretching her limbs, which were stiff from sitting for hours, she went to the window. "It's difficult to concentrate," she muttered. "What with blood about to be spilled."

"Aye," Mairi agreed softly. A rustle of fabric followed as her sister-by-marriage rose to her feet and joined her at the window. Together they watched as men-at-arms hurried across the outer courtyard. Horses whinnied, and urgent male voices called to each other.

Finn strode into view then, his lean form tense with purpose while he shouted something to one of the stable lads who was idling nearby.

Astrid's gaze narrowed as she observed her nemesis. Objectively, she knew the man was attractive. Tall, his lean form clad in close-fitting leathers, he moved with restless energy. His sharp features were set in a determined expression this morning, his hazel gaze narrowed slightly. A breeze ruffled Finn's light-brown hair, which brushed the collar of his fur-edged cloak. He was a man filled with impatience. Astrid didn't think she'd ever seen him relax, not truly.

Her mouth thinned in anticipation of the journey ahead.

"God's blood, how will I suffer him?" she breathed, voicing her thoughts aloud.

"Don't worry, Astrid," Mairi replied after a brief pause. "It won't be as bad as ye think."

Astrid cut her sister-by-marriage an affronted look to see that Mairi was watching her closely. "No," she muttered. "It'll be worse."

"Do ye really hate him that much?"

Astrid inhaled sharply. Although Mairi had been living at Duart for months now, this was the first time she'd directly brought Finn up. Usually, they skirted around him in conversation, and when Astrid made the odd scathing comment, Mairi chose to ignore it.

Not so today though—perhaps Loch's response to their feuding earlier had emboldened her, for she continued to hold Astrid's eye steadily, unbothered by her glare.

"Aye," Astrid admitted after a few moments. "He's a thorn in my side ... one that has festered for years now. Every time I set eyes on him, I remember what he did to Maggie."

Mairi's gaze shadowed at this admission. "Ye loved her very much, didn't ye?"

Astrid nodded, her throat thickening. Even now, over a decade later, grief still welled inside her whenever she thought of her dear friend. "She was the sister I never had," she whispered.

"What was Maggie like?" Mairi asked, placing a gentle hand on Astrid's arm.

Astrid's mouth curved. "She was small and birdlike, with a mop of wild curly brown hair and eyes of the brightest blue ye have ever seen ... and she had a love for adventure." She paused then, her smile fading. "She was a fisherman's daughter though ... and my parents didn't approve of our friendship. I used to sneak away to see her when we were bairns ... I taught her how to ride a pony, and together, we explored the coast."

"So, yer parents grew to accept the two of ye being friends?"

Astrid sighed. "Not really ... but they had their hands full with Loch. He was wild and difficult, and after Jack and Finn's arrival, he got himself into all kinds of trouble. They eventually chose to ignore my friendship with Maggie." Astrid's gaze shifted then, back to the courtyard below, where Finn was now deep in discussion with the new marshal. Her brow furrowed. "But *he* destroyed everything."

Mairi didn't reply to that, and Astrid's mind traveled back, remembering the day she and Maggie had been walking home after visiting the market at Craignure. They'd met Loch, Jack, and Finn on the track. Loch had been dismissive, as usual, and Jack teasing, while Finn had said little. Even then, he'd been someone who gave little away about himself.

However, his gaze had never left Maggie's face as she excitedly told him about the juggler they'd watched at market. Astrid had marked how her friend's cheeks flushed, how she flirted and giggled. Jealousy had spiked through Astrid as she watched them—a complicated sensation, for she didn't like being left out. She'd also known, instinctively, that someone else was about to intrude on the bond she and Maggie shared.

She'd been right. That had been the beginning of things.

And a few months later, Maggie Garvie was dead.

"We'd better get back to work," Astrid said with a sigh. Talking about the past was wearying. It brought everything back to the surface. "Those arrows won't make themselves."

"Aye ... come on." Mairi turned from the window, her hand straying to her midriff.

"Can ye feel the bairn?" Astrid asked, stilling.

Mairi nodded, her eyes wide.

"It's early, isn't it?"

"The midwife said I would be able to feel something around four moons in … and that's where I am," Mairi replied. Her fingers spanned over her midsection, which had yet to show any signs of pregnancy. A smile tugged at her mouth. "I must tell, Loch."

Astrid nodded, flashing her sister-by-marriage an excited smile. "Aye, go to him then."

Mairi moved toward the doorway. "I'll be back soon to help with the rest of the arrows."

"Don't worry, I can finish here," Astrid called after her.

Watching as her sister-by-marriage departed, Astrid thought about Mairi and Loch, and the new life they'd made together. And, despite her worries about what lay ahead, a smile lingered on her lips.

It warmed her soul to see them both so happy.

4: HER SHADOW

PULLING HER CLOAK tightly about her, Astrid trudged through the sand to where the *Sea Eagle* awaited. A few yards back, above the tideline, four other birlinns perched, waiting to depart for Dounarwyse.

Astrid's escort—a crew of fourteen warriors—clustered around the birlinn at the water's edge, their figures ghostly in the mist and drizzle that blanketed the world this morning, while the galley's single mast pierced the fog.

The sun had recently risen, although its friendly face was nowhere to be seen. And the chill air that stung Astrid's face made it difficult to believe it was May. Summer was nearly upon them, yet it was hard not to shiver.

Captain MacDonald's gaze pierced Astrid's as she approached, sweeping over her cloaked form. The wind snagged at her mantle then, pulling it aside for a moment, and Finn's eyes narrowed. Aye, he'd seen the dirk she carried at her hip, and the belt of throwing knives she'd strapped around her waist too.

Astrid raised her chin, daring him to challenge her.

This was *her* mission, and these were dangerous times. As such, she'd travel armed.

Finn's gaze narrowed further, yet he held his tongue.

Usually, it would be the leader of her escort who'd help her onto the ship—not so today though. Finn knew that Astrid would rather touch a leper than take his hand, and so he stepped back when she reached the galley, allowing Dougie, one of his men, to move to Astrid's side.

Finn's behavior didn't surprise her. It seemed that he was as reluctant to touch her as she was him.

Seated at the stern, only a couple of feet from the steering oar, Astrid waited while her escort heaved the galley properly into the water. The warriors then clambered onboard and took their places. Moments later, they were off, churning through the surf as the oarsmen propelled them out into Duart Bay itself.

Spindrift and misty rain coated Astrid's face, and the briny scent of the sea filled her lungs as she gripped onto the sides. She'd accompanied her father on many journeys over the years and usually found the trips exhilarating. Nonetheless, rough seas tended to make her a little nervous.

They moved out into the bay, and Astrid craned her neck to look up at the cliffs above. The wreathing mist nearly obscured the castle this morning, its high curtain wall disappearing into the murk.

Astrid's belly clenched as worry about what the future held swept over her, and she whispered a prayer. The outer courtyard had already been full of men and horses when they'd departed—Loch in the midst of it all, organizing last-minute details.

Astrid wasn't the only one leaving this morning. Her brother was about to lead his force of sixty warriors north, to join the Macleans of Dounarwyse. Some would travel by birlinn, while others would make the journey on horseback. Loch had already sent out riders to Moy and Croggan, and a boat to Breachacha. More of their clansmen would shortly be on their way, but in the meantime, Dounarwyse couldn't stand alone.

Misgiving stole over Astrid then.

Despite that her brother was a warrior of renown, who'd led men into battle countless times against the English, a tight knot formed in her belly.

It wasn't just the upcoming conflict that worried her, but something else.

When Finn had returned from Dounarwyse back in March, with the news that he'd left Jack and Tara there—he'd also brought stranger, more discomforting news.

It seemed that while Jack had been dragging his captive across the isle, he'd spied a specter in the shadow of the great mountain Ben More.

The Headless Horseman had galloped across his path—a man dressed in flowing black upon a black steed, a bloody stump where his head should have been.

Of course, like everyone who'd grown up on Mull, Astrid knew the tale of the warrior who'd lost his head during battle and now roamed the area west of Ben More, seeking his rightful place as chieftain—but secretly, she'd thought it was just a tale.

According to her cousin, it wasn't. Legend had it that if a Maclean witnessed The Headless Horseman, it was an omen that one of his family would shortly die.

A chill prickled Astrid's skin. The Macleans of Duart and Dounarwyse were blood kin. Loch and Astrid were cousins to Rae and Jack. She'd worried about Loch ever since. Of course, it could have been any of the four of them, but for some reason, her mind had seized on her brother, and it wouldn't let go.

All the more reason why she had to make haste to Skye and ensure that the Macleans of Mull didn't stand alone against their foe.

She couldn't let her brother, or her clan, down.

Exhaling slowly, Astrid pushed worries about Loch aside and tore her gaze from her beloved castle. Her attention slid over the twelve oarsmen who moved in unison, to two men, Finn and another, unfurling the sail.

Out here on the water, a breeze picked up. The *Sea Eagle* was a swift craft, built for speed, unlike some of the bigger galleys. The heavy woven wool sail snapped and then billowed, catching the wind, and, rigging creaking, the birlinn lurched forward. Keeping a tight hold on the railing, Astrid watched as Finn left his companion to trim the sail while he picked his way down, between the oarsmen, to the stern.

Astrid's mouth thinned as he approached. She'd hoped he'd keep his distance during the journey, yet it seemed he wouldn't.

However, the captain didn't acknowledge her. Indeed, his gaze moved right past Astrid, as if she weren't even there, as he squeezed by and took his place at the steering oar.

And as he moved past her—closer to her than he'd ever been—Astrid inhaled his scent: leather with a woodsy, sharp undertone that reminded her of a pinewood in summer. And despite herself, Astrid had to admit that it was a pleasant smell, one that calmed her breathing and eased her nerves. It certainly wasn't what she'd have expected of her enemy.

Her mouth compressed as she inwardly chastised herself. *What did ye expect, lass? For him to smell of iron and sulfur like the devil?*

Finn shifted the steering oar slightly, angling the birlinn farther east than he usually would as they traveled up the Sound of Mull. The last time they'd sailed north, they'd hugged the eastern coast of the Isle of Mull and watched the wind-blasted cliffs slide by before Dounarwyse broch itself hove into view.

However, it was risky to go anywhere near the coast this morning. The Mackinnons and their allies would be there—and it was imperative that the enemy didn't spot the *Sea Eagle*. Finn had been vexed at dawn, upon spying the mist, although in many ways it was their ally. It had masked their departure, and now that it was clearing slightly, he was able to navigate the birlinn without worrying that he'd accidentally run the vessel aground.

His early years amongst his kin, on the Isle of Islay, had taught Finn much about the sea. All his family were seafarers; his uncle was a merchant who'd sailed the entire coast of Scotland, and he always returned with exciting tales.

Finn's jaw tightened at the thought of his childhood on Islay, bitterness souring his mouth. His parents had sent him away when he was seven, and he'd never been home since. He hadn't had any contact with his parents or his elder brothers over the years. None of his family had visited him at Duart, or sent word, in the years he fostered there, and in response, he'd turned his back on them.

Islay hadn't been his home for a long while.

Finn's mouth thinned. These days, he wasn't sure where he belonged.

Aye, he served Loch now, but he was a MacDonald of Dunnyveg, not a Maclean of Duart. Blood was blood, after all. It didn't matter how many years he lived on Mull, he'd always be the lad who'd fostered at Duart and never left.

Finn cut a glance to the woman seated just a foot from him—so close he could have reached out and touched her. It surprised him she'd defied her brother and turned up this morning with enough steel on her to bring down a charging boar. However, Loch was too preoccupied with war to worry about his sister bearing weapons.

Pulling a face, Finn looked away from Astrid.

No, Duart wasn't home either, especially since he wasn't well-liked there, but his loyalty to Loch and Jack was everything to him. His two friends were the only people in this cesspit of a world he really cared about, but even they couldn't erase the past.

The reality was that Maggie's death had left a lasting scar upon Duart and Craignure, and he'd forever be known as 'the beast who drowned that poor lass'.

Finn's grip tightened upon the steering oar, and despite himself, he glanced Astrid's way once more. She was staring north, her chin held high, her gaze slightly narrowed. Her profile was both delicate and proud. Strands of pale-blonde hair had come free of her braid and stuck to her cheeks, for the rain continued to fall in a silent mist.

It was hard to believe such a lovely creature had become his archenemy. This woman made it impossible for him to move forward with his life. Wherever he went, she was always there, her peat-brown eyes damning him. And thanks to the vicious harpy, the locals would never let the past go. Many of the fisherfolk still muttered under their breaths and cast him dark looks whenever he ventured into Craignure.

It was as if Astrid had made it her mission to never let him forget Maggie.

As if he ever could.

Pressure rose under Finn's breastbone then, his resentment giving way to another, more uncomfortable, emotion. The young woman's final moments would be etched on his memory until the end of his days.

Although the mist eventually cleared, the wind grew sharp and cold as the day progressed. Astrid was grateful for the thick fur cloak she'd donned for the journey. It cocooned her from the worst of the chill. However, by the time they reached Sanna—a hamlet perched upon the far western tip of the Ardnamurchan peninsula, where they'd stay overnight—her fingers were numb and her face chapped.

It was a relief when the men angled the birlinn for the shore, their oars cutting through the surf toward a wide sandy beach. Above, a collection of crofts perched on the emerald-green headland—a welcoming sight indeed.

Once they reached the shallows, Finn and his men leaped over the side of the galley and pushed it onto the beach. And there, once again, the captain stepped aside, to let one of his men—a warrior named Colin, this time—help Astrid down from the birlinn.

Ever since departing Duart, neither Astrid nor Finn had acknowledged each other—and if Astrid had her way, she wouldn't speak to him during the entire journey.

Even so, to her annoyance, Astrid was always aware of his presence. He'd taken the steering oar at the stern a few times during the day, often brushing close to her to sit down, for the space was narrow. And each time, the scent of leather and pine filled her nostrils. And now, as she picked up her skirts and trudged up onto the sand, Astrid knew without looking over her shoulder that Finn was just a couple of strides behind her.

Loch had charged him with her protection, and he'd do as ordered.

Astrid clenched her jaw, bristling at his proximity. God's teeth, how would she weather having this man as her shadow over the coming days?

The warriors heaved the birlinn above the tideline and tied down the sail before the party of fifteen climbed the hill to the tiny hamlet. Astrid had done her best to pack as little as possible to bring with her—nonetheless, two of the men carried her leather satchels slung across their fronts. Dusk was settling now, turning the already grey day darker still.

On the outskirts of the village, a woman of middling age with a careworn face and a warm smile met the newcomers as they approached.

"Welcome, travelers," she greeted them, her gaze roaming over the party before coming to rest on Astrid. "Are ye looking for lodgings for the night?"

"Aye, can ye provide some?" Finn asked before Astrid could answer.

The woman nodded. "As ye can see, our village is too small for an inn … however, I have a barn behind my cottage that will keep ye warm and dry overnight." She paused then, her gaze never leaving Astrid. Curiosity gleamed in her eyes.

"Apologies, Captain MacDonald has forgotten his manners," Astrid murmured, ignoring the glare Finn cut her as she stepped forward. "I'm Lady Astrid Maclean, sister to the clan-chief of the Macleans of Duart." She gestured to the men surrounding her then. "My men and I are bound for Skye and would indeed appreciate yer lodgings."

The woman's smile widened. "Four silver pennies will give ye a bed each and a meal of roast mutton and ale," she replied.

"Agreed." Astrid nodded before digging into the purse she wore upon her belt and extracting the fee.

Their hostess beamed at her, tucked the coins into her bodice, and then stepped back, motioning for them to follow. "This way."

She led them around her stone cottage, with its rambling garden encircled by a moss-encrusted wall, to where a stone and timber barn had been built into the lee of the hill. Inside, lanterns burned on the walls and a lump of peat glowed upon a central fire pit. The ruddy light revealed a small platform, nestled under heavy crisscrossing beams. "That space is reserved for our lady guests," the woman informed Astrid, motioning to the ladder that led up to the platform. "It's only fitting that ye have a bower of yer own, Lady Astrid."

Astrid smiled at this, relief flooding through her. Indeed, she'd been a little concerned that she wouldn't have much privacy tonight.

"I will return shortly with yer suppers," their hostess said as she bustled toward the door.

Astrid watched her go and then turned to Dougie and Norris, the warriors who carried her bags, favoring them with a smile. "Ye can take them upstairs."

The men nodded and moved to obey. However, to her annoyance, Finn stepped forward as the two warriors climbed the ladder to the platform. "Ye should have let me deal with that." His hazel eyes pinned her to the spot, his lip curling. "That woman fleeced ye."

5: HIS PLACE

ASTRID STIFFENED. "EXCUSE me?"

"Ye should have paid half of what she's charging."

Astrid pursed her lips. "That's yer opinion, MacDonald," she said, her tone as wintry as the anger that now burned in her belly. How typical that the cur had held his tongue all day, only to insult her in front of the others now. "Not mine."

"It's not opinion but fact," he replied, a challenge glinting in his eyes. "Although I suppose ye wouldn't know ... *sheltered* as ye are."

Silence followed this comment.

Astrid was aware that the others of her escort were looking on, observing their captain's disrespect. As always, her first instinct was to go for his throat.

She'd never forget the incident a few months earlier—and neither likely would he—where she'd thrown a sharp eating knife at Finn after he insulted her. They'd been in Loch's solar, and her brother had been horrified at how close she'd come to killing his friend. But her brother's fury had been worth it, just to see the shock that rippled across Finn's face.

She'd have liked to stun Finn again—anything to wipe that arrogance off his face. However, there was no place for outbursts of temper on this mission. She wouldn't lower herself to his level either by insulting him in return. Instead, she would treat Finn with the same cold disdain he reserved for her. It was time she reminded him of his place.

"I may be sheltered, but I'm not stupid," she replied, her gaze never leaving his, even as her pulse thumped in her ears. "And if I wish to hand over a *bag* of silver for a night's accommodation, I shall. Don't question me again."

With that, she turned and moved away, unslinging her cloak from about her shoulders, and hanging it upon a peg on the wall. Then, still ignoring Finn, she took a seat by the fire.

"They're bonnie lodgings to be sure, Lady Astrid," Colin spoke up eventually, shattering the brittle silence. "And it's good to be out of the rain and wind."

Astrid cast the warrior—who hailed from a farming family a short ride south of Duart—a grateful smile. "Aye," she agreed, warming her tingling fingers over the fire. "Let's hope the weather improves for tomorrow's journey."

All the while, she was aware of Finn's baleful glare, yet she pointedly ignored him.

Her chilled fingers started to warm under the fire's glow, and she released a soft sigh.

"We could do without the rain," Colin agreed. "Although we need a brisk wind to carry us north." Their journey the following day would take them across the sea, past the Small Isles, and along the western coast of Skye. There, they'd travel up to Dunvegan, which sat on the northwestern coast of the lobster-shaped isle.

If the wind was favorable, they'd reach Dunvegan by nightfall—and if not, they'd have to break their journey.

Astrid's pulse skittered as she considered this possibility. Time was of the essence now. *Loch will be fighting the Mackinnons.*

Her breathing grew shallow then, fear clutching her throat as she imagined the clash between the two clans. She'd lost both her parents, and her closeness with her brother was new indeed. Despite that she was still sore at Loch's insistence Finn accompany her, the thought of losing him tied her up in knots.

Loch was depending on her to reach the Macleods of Skye swiftly, and to bring back help to Dounarwyse as quickly as possible.

Any delay would cost him.

The door to the barn creaked open then, and their hostess appeared, bearing a large platter, piled high with trenchers of food. The rich, oily aroma of mutton drifted through the barn, and Astrid's belly rumbled. She didn't often have much of an appetite, but after a day at sea, she was starving. Nonetheless, the men who spent long hours at the oars would be even hungrier.

Three comely lasses followed the woman, and judging from their features, they were the woman's daughters—how she would have looked before a hard life took its toll on her face and body. The lasses carried more food as well as cups and ewers of ale.

They were a merry group, laughing and flirting with the men as they served them.

One of them, possibly the prettiest, even roused a half-smile from Finn as she handed him a trencher of mutton and coarse oaten bread. He sat across the fire pit, at the farthest point away from Astrid, so she hadn't heard what the lass said—yet whatever it was had amused him.

Finn's mouth quirked, and for an instant, his sharp-featured face transformed. He murmured something back, eyes glinting, and the lass giggled.

Astrid's mouth pursed, and she cut her glance away. Hades, lasses could be daft. *She'd* never giggled over a man— and certainly not *that* man.

She wasn't that kind of woman. Astrid liked to be taken seriously. When her father's health had declined, she'd discovered she had a skill for leadership. She'd stridden upon the castle walls with a dirk at her hip and had made decisions for the good of her clan. The servants and the Guard respected her.

A chatelaine couldn't act like a witless goose and keep everyone's respect.

Maggie used to giggle over lads.

An ache rose under Astrid's breastbone then, at the memory of how Maggie's blue eyes would sparkle when she was amused. Unlike her friend, Astrid had always been shy about showing her interest in someone. If she was honest, flirting represented a loss of control. It made her feel vulnerable.

Finn took a bite of mutton and chewed slowly. The food was good, he'd admit—although Astrid had paid a king's ransom for it.

Swallowing, he picked up his cup of ale and took a gulp. Around him, his men were bantering and laughing. However, Finn was content to let the conversation eddy around him, to observe rather than participate.

He'd always been an observer. Always on the outside looking in.

He preferred it that way.

His gaze shifted then, across the glowing fire pit, to where Astrid sat, eating her supper. After her illness months earlier, the lass had been painfully thin—so fragile that it looked as if a gust of wind could blow her away. But these days, she was looking far healthier. Her cheeks had filled out, and the waifish lines of her body had gotten fuller. She devoured her meat and bread hungrily as she listened to the conversation between the warriors closest to her.

Finn's mouth pursed as he observed the laird's sister.

Don't question me again.

He'd swallowed his ire earlier and literally bitten his tongue to stop himself from replying. However, anger still simmered within him in the aftermath. How he longed to cut the high and mighty chit down. *He* was leading this mission, not her. If he decided to question Astrid, he would.

They weren't so different in rank. He was a chieftain's son, after all. And yet, she'd treated him like a baseborn cur.

He wouldn't forget it.

"How about a game of knucklebones, Captain?" Dougie's voice roused him from thoughts of revenge, and Finn cut his gaze to the red-haired and freckled warrior seated to his right. Dougie hailed from Craignure. A fisherman's son, he'd upset his family by choosing the warrior's path instead. However, Finn was glad he'd joined the Duart Guard, for the lad was one of his best.

"Ready for me to wipe the floor with ye again, are ye?" Finn challenged, putting down his trencher and reaching for the pouch at his belt.

Dougie snorted a laugh. "I've been practicing, ye know?"

Finn raised an eyebrow. "Aye?"

"Aye." One of the other warriors, a big broad man named Roy called out. "Dougie beat me two days ago."

Finn snorted. "That's hardly a challenge."

Roy flashed him a toothy grin and heaved himself off his stool. "Right ... I'm joining ye for a game." He swept his gaze over the rest of the group. "Which of ye lads thinks ye can beat our captain?"

Murmurs and muttering followed, and Roy harrumphed. "Come on ... someone has to wipe that smirk off MacDonald's face."

Finn cocked an eyebrow. They could try, but all his men knew he was a fiend at knucklebones. Lord knows, he'd practiced often enough, for when he'd been on campaign, following the Bruce across Scotland, there had always been someone keen for a game in the evenings.

"I shall play," a cool female voice replied. "If I'm permitted, of course."

All gazes, including Finn's, cut to where Lady Astrid observed them.

There was no mistaking the challenge in her dark-brown eyes, and when her attention shifted to Finn, her face hardened.

Finn fought the urge to make a mocking remark. There was a part of him that wanted to dismiss her, to put the woman in her place as she'd done with him earlier.

But his men's faces were now expectant. They all liked the laird's daughter, respected her. He wouldn't win any friends tonight by putting her down. And he had to admit that her behavior intrigued him. He'd never seen her play knucklebones. Indeed, women usually left their menfolk to such pastimes.

"Very well, Lady Astrid," he drawled, jerking his head toward the trestle table behind him. "Let's get started."

6: A GAME OF KNUCKLEBONES

ASTRID WATCHED THE first of their group take his turn with the knucklebones, observing the flick of his wrist as he scattered the yellowed bones, which were shiny with use, across the pitted wooden surface between them. There were eleven playing pieces—one of which was used as the jack.

Dougie then set about throwing one of the knucklebones into the air before scooping up a bone from the table at a time and catching the jack before it fell. He did this easily, working his way across the table methodically. He then threw the bone into the air once more, repeating the move, but scooping up two this time.

The other players, Astrid included, looked on in silence as Dougie continued. There was something hypnotic about watching a game of knucklebones unfold. Dougie's cheeks were flushed with ale and the warmth of the fire, and he was looking pleased with himself, as if, indeed, he had been practicing.

The young warrior got all the way up to five before he missed. This was tricky, as the player had to scoop up half the bones in the first go and the other half in the second. Dougie managed the first five, but when he attempted to scoop up the remaining bones, they slipped from his fingers, scattering across the tabletop.

He muttered a curse, his green eyes narrowing, while around him, some of the other players whooped.

"Four isn't bad, lad," Roy said, slapping him on the back. "My turn now though."

Astrid continued to observe with interest. The knucklebones were good-sized, and the most one could pick up was ten. Her hands were much smaller than those of the men she was playing with, so she was at a disadvantage.

Dougie had indeed done well, for four was the most any of them managed.

And then Finn took his turn.

As much as it galled Astrid to admit it, the bastard was uncommonly skilled. He was lightning fast as he collected ones, twos, threes, and fours with ease. And when he managed fives as well, her breathing slowed.

How far would he go?

Finn's gaze narrowed as he scooped up the first four knucklebones he'd scattered across the table. The remaining six lay spread out, too far for most folk to gather while the jack was in the air.

Astrid swallowed a smile. There was no way he'd manage it.

But he did, tossing the jack high while sweeping his hand gracefully across the table, gathering the knucklebones as he went. Then, with a flick of his wrist, he caught the jack.

Next to Astrid, Roy murmured an oath.

"Keep going then," Dougie muttered, grudging respect in his voice. "Let's see if ye can manage seven."

Finn's mouth lifted at the corners as he flipped the knucklebones, allowing them to rattle over the table while one remained balanced on the back of his hand—the jack. He gathered up the first three with ease.

He hesitated then, his gaze sliding over the remaining seven, which lay far and wide over the table surface.

Astrid couldn't help it, she gave a soft snort. "Think ye can do it, MacDonald?"

His gaze flicked up, fusing with hers. "Aye."

He tossed the jack high then and attempted to scoop up the seven—but unfortunately for him, his fingertips brushed one of the bones, sending it skittering onto the floor.

Finn had caught six rather than seven.

Astrid crossed her arms over her chest and allowed herself a smirk.

Her nemesis, on the other hand, looked vexed. Even when Colin and Norris, who were seated on either side of him, slapped him on the back and told him he'd played well, the sour look on his face didn't ease.

Finn clearly wasn't a man who liked to lose.

His attention shifted to Astrid once more, a challenge glinting in his eyes. "Yer turn, *my lady.*"

Astrid nodded, even as her pulse quickened.

She marked the amused looks some of the warriors shared then, their expressions of masculine indulgence.

"Go on, Lady Astrid." Dougie gave her an encouraging smile. "Show them how it's done."

Astrid smiled back at him, grateful for the support. She'd always liked Dougie.

However, one of the men watching their game muttered under his breath. "She won't get past twos."

Astrid's smile faded, and she cut the warrior a sharp look. "We'll see about that."

Indeed, unbeknown to her companions, she'd played this game before. Many times.

Picking up the knucklebones, she tested their weight in her hand, listening to the reassuring 'click' as they rattled together.

Nervousness fluttered up then. It had been nearly a year since she'd played last, and she was likely a little rusty.

Just take it easy, she counseled herself. *Don't rush.*

Astrid began to play, taking her time.

Nonetheless, as she completed ones, twos, and threes without a hitch, the expressions around her sobered.

Satisfaction suffused Astrid when she saw their faces— there was nothing better than putting men in their place when they underestimated her.

Astrid didn't look Finn's way as she played though, for the man had a stare that could pierce iron. She didn't want to be distracted.

She completed fours and then went on to fives. It was getting trickier now. But although her palms weren't as big as her competitors', she had long nimble fingers that aided her.

Murmurs rumbled through the barn when she caught the second lot of fives.

"She'll never get through sixes," Colin murmured under his breath, voicing his thoughts aloud without thinking.

Astrid cut him an arch look. "I heard that, Colin."

The warrior flushed. "Sorry, Lady Astrid."

Her mouth curved. "Aye, well ... let's see if I can prove ye wrong."

And she did, just barely—scooping up the final six with a dexterous move she'd spent years practicing.

The men around her whooped, grins stretching their faces.

However, Finn wasn't smiling. Instead, he met her eye, his expression veiled, before asking, "Who taught ye to play?"

"My father," she replied.

Finn's hazel eyes widened at this, as if he didn't believe her. Yet it was the truth. After her mother died, father and daughter had sat together in the long summer's eves in his solar, with a cup of wine at their elbows, and played for hours. Iain Maclean had been excellent at knucklebones, with quick reflexes that never dulled, even as he aged. He'd taught Astrid all his tricks too.

She hadn't played since his death, and indeed, the sight of others playing the game often made sadness tighten her chest. However, Finn's arrogance had goaded her into speaking up.

To beat him and see the look on his face would be a prize indeed.

The bastard would choke on his own tongue.

And she was close to doing so now. If she completed sevens, she'd be the winner.

Her pulse sped up, anxiety eroding her confidence.

Sevens was tricky, as Finn had demonstrated. It would all depend on where the bones fell.

Much to her disappointment, they scattered far—not as far as Finn's had, yet wide enough to make this round a challenge.

Astrid scooped up the first three on the left. She was using her right hand so those closest to her would be easier to leave. After that, she studied the remaining seven for a few moments.

Then, drawing in a deep breath, she tossed the jack high—higher than usual—before sweeping her hand in an arc over the remaining pieces. And to her joy, she scooped them all up.

Only to drop the jack.

It pinged off the table just an inch away from her hand.

Groans and oaths followed, echoing up into the rafters. It seemed that after being skeptical of her skill at the beginning of her turn, the others had all been hoping she'd trounce Finn.

Astrid bit back a curse. Failure was a bitter gall.

She'd been so close.

Trying her best to mask her disappointment, she straightened up on her stool. And all the while, she could feel

Finn's gaze boring into her, daring her to look his way. After a heartbeat, she succumbed. She wasn't about to let him intimidate her.

She'd expected to see a smirk on his face, yet his expression was inscrutable.

"It's a tie then," he said, ignoring the exuberance of the men seated around them. The warriors were now ribbing each other and readying themselves for another game.

Reluctantly, Astrid nodded. "Ye play well," she admitted, determined not to appear a poor loser. "Who taught ye?"

His gaze never left hers as he answered, "Yer father."

They all retired early, for the next day's journey would be a long one, and Finn wanted his men fresh.

Wrapping himself in his fur-lined cloak, Finn took his place upon a sheepskin by the fire. And as he did so, he spared a glance up at the platform, where Astrid had retired.

He and his men had indulged in another two games of knucklebones, but she'd left them to it, climbing the ladder and disappearing into the shadows upstairs.

Finn caught a glimmer of pale hair yet could see nothing else. He wagered the lady was fast asleep. Nothing tired a person out more than a day at sea. They'd all be exhausted by the time they reached Dunvegan, but they couldn't afford to break the trip up into three days as most travelers would.

All day, Finn had been keenly aware of the passing of time, and as he stretched out onto his back, his gaze going to the heavy rafters above, he wondered how Loch and Jack were faring.

Loch and his warriors would have engaged the Mackinnons today, likely outside the walls, while Jack was in charge of holding the broch against the enemy.

Frustration quickened within Finn then.

He wanted to be with his friends, fighting at their side. Aye, this mission was crucial, yet he chafed at being Lady Astrid's escort. His skills were better used back on Mull—although Loch clearly thought otherwise.

Grinding his teeth, Finn glanced once more up at the platform.

He couldn't help it, for Astrid had surprised him this evening. He hadn't realized that Iain Maclean had taught them *both* how to play knucklebones, and the discovery oddly felt like a betrayal of sorts. Worse still, Astrid was skilled and displayed single-minded determination as she played.

The lass had a will of iron and was just as stubborn as he was.

Finn scowled then, yanking his gaze away from where his archenemy slept. *We're nothing alike*, he corrected himself. *She's a vindictive, ill-tempered shrew.*

Aye, but she played knucklebones like a master.

Over the years, Finn had beaten many people at the game and drawn with only a few. Even fewer had beaten him, yet he knew that Astrid was capable of it.

And despite that the sight of the woman cramped his guts, there was another, treacherous, part of him that longed to play another game with her.

7: INTO THE DEEP

ASTRID FROWNED WHEN she spied the storm clouds looming to the west.

They'd set off from Sanna with the first blush of dawn, with a brisk wind filling the birlinn's sail. Once again, Astrid had been grateful for her thick cloak, for the wind, which gusted in from the west, had teeth.

But those clouds on the horizon had an ominous look, and as they boiled closer, they seemed to grow darker, almost purple, in hue.

Still frowning, Astrid twisted on her seat, her gaze shifting to where Finn gripped the steering oar. "There's a storm coming," she informed him. "We should find a safe haven."

His mouth twisted, his eyes narrowing slightly. "Already noted," he replied, raising his voice to be heard as a particularly vicious gust barreled into them. "I'm already steering us toward the Isle of Rùm."

Astrid cut her attention east, hoping to see the shadow of land on the horizon, yet they were still surrounded by water. Misgiving feathered through her then. They were in the midst of the sea now, having sailed past the Isle of Muck, the first of the Small Isles, around an hour earlier. She didn't like not being able to see land, especially with those threatening clouds racing toward them.

A loss of control, a sense of vulnerability, quickened her breathing and chilled her limbs.

Likewise, the faces of the men surrounding her were grim. The sky had been clear when they'd set off, yet the weather had taken a turn. The seas off the west coast of Scotland could be perilous, all sailors knew that, but May was usually a safe enough month to travel between the isles.

Astrid's belly clenched as she turned her focus back to Finn. "Will we make it in time?"

His lean face tensed. "I thought we would," he muttered. "But judging from how fast those clouds are moving, I think the storm will hit us before we reach Rùm."

Astrid tightened her hold on the plank where she was sitting. Murmuring an oath, she looked west, wishing a glare would send those clouds scurrying away. But of course, that was a foolish hope.

Moments later, the sea around them grew choppy and whitecaps appeared. The birlinn, which was at full sail now, angled through the waves, helped by the oarsmen who propelled it forward. The *Sea Eagle* was flying, yet it wasn't fleet enough to outrun the coming storm.

It wasn't long afterward that a shadow fell across the sea, angry purple and slate clouds closed in, and the storm hit them like a mailed fist.

Astrid thought she knew what fear was—but as the storm howled around them, she tasted true terror.

Clinging with one hand to the side of the galley, the other to her seat, she bit down on her tongue to stop herself from screaming—so hard that she tasted the iron tang of blood.

Finn hadn't changed course. They were still heading for the Isle of Rùm. But with the storm on all sides now, it was impossible to see more than a few yards in any direction.

The waves grew to the size of hills, dwarfing the twelve-oar birlinn as it climbed a dark, glossy slope. The galley perched on the brow of that watery promontory, teetering there in midair for a few heartbeats, before it plunged down into the valley below.

The motion was so swift that it left Astrid's belly behind her. She couldn't help it. A scream tore from her throat. However, the roar of the wind and sea drowned out the noise.

The faces of her escort, pinched and pale, betrayed their own fear; yet they still tried to row their way through the storm. It was useless though, for the tempest had them in its claws.

Up and down they went—and they were barreling down a particularly steep trough when one of the oarsmen toppled over the side into the churning water.

Astrid screamed again, horror washing over her as Norris's dark head went under the water.

Next to her, Finn spat out a curse and lurched forward. He then leaned over the side, with Roy grabbing his legs, and tried to catch hold of the man overboard. But the sea had sucked Norris under, and as the birlinn climbed the next hill, they didn't see him again.

Astrid twisted around, a sob clutching at her breast as she fixed on the spot where Norris had disappeared. She couldn't believe the sea had taken him. Panicked shouts from the other crew members rose and fell around her.

Tears scalded Astrid's chilled, wind-chapped face while they climbed to the summit of another great wave.

Norris was her age. They'd grown up together in the keep. He was the son of one of the grooms, a big-hearted lad everyone liked. And now he was gone.

Panic assailed her then, fear swirling in a wild vortex inside her chest. Her heart was beating so hard now she feared it might stop, and crippling despair—a sensation that reminded her of how she'd felt after her failed escape months earlier—barreled into her.

They were all done for. There was no way out of this.

The *Sea Eagle* dove once more, heading toward another terrifying trough—and this time, an ominous 'crack' clove through the howling wind and roar of water.

The mast had just snapped in two, and as it fell, the heavy sail billowed and the rigging creaked and pinged as it gave way.

Three of the oarsmen tried, foolishly, to save the mast. They launched themselves toward it, grabbing hold of the tough woven wool. But it merely yanked them off the galley and into the churning water.

The sight of the men struggling in the sea pulled Astrid out of the claws of despair. Without thinking, she lunged forward to help them. However, a strong arm looped around her belly and hauled her back.

"Stay seated," Finn growled in her ear, "or it'll be ye who goes over next."

Astrid rounded on him, driving her elbow into his belly as she fought to get free. "Let me go, knave! We have to help them!"

"Aye," he grunted. "We will ... but *ye* will sit down and hold tight. That's an order."

Heart pounding, she relented. Finn released her then, moving past her as he tossed a coil of rope out to the flailing warriors.

One of them, Colin, caught it, and was just about to haul himself back toward the galley, when the sail billowed down over the top of him.

Finn swore viciously as he, along with Dougie, tried to yank the sail away so they could get to the men in the water.

Dougie was shouting their names, his voice raw with fear.

The same fear that pulsed like a stoked ember inside Astrid now, fusing her to the spot. She'd had a moment of foolish bravery earlier, when she'd moved to help Colin and the others, but now terror seized her once more.

Her limbs felt cold and dead. She couldn't move.

A wave crashed over the boat then, sending an avalanche of freezing water over them. The impact of it hitting Astrid was like striking a wall.

She'd been clinging onto the side, but her grip wasn't strong enough to withstand the impact. The wave knocked her over the side, and then she was being pulled underwater.

Panic kicked her in the chest, and suddenly her limbs worked again. She clawed her way upward, breaking the surface and heaving in a deep breath.

The boat was just yards away, yet to her horror, it was breaking up, and sinking into the whirling, churning maelstrom in the base of the trough. On either side, dark, gleaming walls of water rose up overhead.

They were trapped in a watery abyss with no way out.

Finn appeared over the edge of the birlinn then, grappling with the side as he looked wildly around.

"Finn!" she screamed, panic pulsing inside her.

Hearing his name, he looked her way, and their gazes fused for an instant.

And then another wave swept over them, blinding Astrid and dragging her under.

Clawing her way to the surface once more, she found herself alone. Where was the *Sea Eagle*? Where was the rest of her party?

"Finn!" she screamed, desperately trying to keep afloat as the water tried to suck her down. She'd learned to swim as a bairn, but it was difficult to fight this churning sea.

"Over here!" A voice rasped from behind her.

Astrid turned to see Finn clinging to a large plank of wood. His hair was plastered against his skull, his eyes were wide, and his face was taut. He then kicked, pushing himself and the plank toward her. "Grab ahold."

With a sob of relief, she lurched toward him, grabbing onto the flotsam, just as another wave hit them.

The piece of the birlinn's hull kept them afloat in the churning water. When they were able to see once more, Astrid looked wildly around her, blinking salt water out of her stinging eyes. "Where are the others?"

"Nearby ... we just can't see them."

"But we—"

Waves swept over them once more, and Astrid choked on a mouthful of briny water. Wheezing and spluttering, she clung to the plank, misery twisting inside her.

The storm had destroyed the *Sea Eagle*. The crew were all in the water. How many of them had already drowned?

A sob caught in her throat, yet she choked it back.

No, she couldn't let hysteria take over. She wanted to find the others, to help them, but the truth was that she too was in grave danger right now.

"Just keep ahold of the plank," Finn ordered. His face was slick with water, his features even sharper than usual as his gaze fused with hers. "It's the only thing that'll save ye."

Astrid clenched her jaw tight and nodded. She wasn't in the habit of doing anything this man told her. But right now, as the storm howled its fury, and they bobbed like two corks on the wild sea, her enemy was the only thing between her and a watery death.

8: IN HER ENEMY'S ARMS

THEY WERE IN deep trouble.

The storm had come upon them fast, and as soon as he'd spied those ominous clouds, Finn made for the Isle of Rùm. But he hadn't been quick enough. And now, his entire crew had been tossed overboard, and the ravenous sea had just swallowed the *Sea Eagle* into its maw.

It had taken them all. And even as Finn peered around him, trying to penetrate the sea spray and curtains of slashing rain, grief twisted his guts.

His men. Some of them must have caught pieces of the flotsam when the birlinn broke apart.

He had to believe that just beyond the walls of water that hemmed him and Astrid in, they were clinging on for their lives as well.

Dragging his attention back to his own predicament, Finn looked over at the laird's sister.

Astrid's face was pale and drawn, her dark eyes huge.

Her terror was palpable, and he didn't blame her. Right now, it took everything he had to cling to his own courage. There were few things more frightening than being in the midst of a storm at sea. Water had such power, and now it was in a terrible rage.

Finn's gaze fused with Astrid's.

For the first time in over a decade, they didn't glare at each other. Things were too desperate for them to focus on anything except the fact they were adrift in a wild sea, with no land in sight.

Astrid's breast heaved as she clung to the oaken plank, and Finn realized she was struggling to rein in panic.

"Slow yer breathing," he shouted above the roar of the storm. "Just concentrate on holding on."

Her throat bobbed, her eyes glistening now, yet she managed a nod.

They continued to grip their precious liferaft, riding the swells as the storm raged around them. Finn stopped speaking; he was too intent on staying afloat. At this point, he'd lost all sense of direction. He couldn't see the sun or anything else that would allow him to orient himself.

Instead, he had no choice but to ride each swell and wait out the storm.

For a while, it seemed as if it would never end—and then, through his exhaustion, Finn was dimly aware that the wind wasn't quite so loud, the waves quite so high.

He was tiring fast now though, and his fingers were cramped and numb from holding on. He couldn't feel his body either. Opposite, Astrid was shivering. Not a good sign. If they didn't get out of the water soon, they'd both die of cold. Aye, it was May, and the water wasn't as gelid as in the winter months—but they'd been in it too long.

And then, when they crested yet another swell, he caught sight of something dark off to his left.

Relief swooped through Finn, and he almost sobbed. "Land!" he croaked.

Astrid didn't respond. Her eyes were glazed now as she retreated into her own world.

"Land!" he shouted, his voice raw from the salt water.

Her gaze lifted, realization dawning upon her face.

Even though his body was numb, Finn roused the last of his strength, clenched his jaw hard, and started to kick out toward the rocks that beckoned.

Astrid began to weep when she spied the wind-blasted headland drawing close. She didn't know where they'd washed up, and she didn't care.

All that mattered was that she was alive.

She didn't even protest when Finn picked her up in the shallows and carried her onto the sandy beach. He was staggering, as if drunk, and barely managed the journey either. Wrapping her arms about his neck, Astrid clung to him.

Christ's blood, she was so cold. She couldn't stop trembling.

Out of the water, the wind was equally chill, made worse by their wet clothing.

She thought Finn might set her down on the sand, but he didn't. Instead, he carried her up, above the tideline and over the dunes, to where a cave opened up under the cliff face.

Halfway there, he fell to his knees.

His rasped curse echoed in Astrid's ear, his breath feathering across her cheek. He then heaved himself up and staggered on, only setting her down once they were inside the mouth of the cave, out of the biting wind.

Astrid collapsed upon the ground, spreading her numb fingers across the solid stone floor, and silently thanking the Lord for delivering her from the storm. How good it felt to be on land again, for the horizon to be steady.

A sob welled then, clawing its way up from her belly.

The beach they'd alighted upon was empty. There was no sign of the others who'd been shipwrecked—the thirteen warriors who'd accompanied them north.

Had they all perished?

Astrid clenched her eyes shut, even as hot tears stung them.

How would they reach Skye in time now?

Loch would have already engaged the enemy, and he wouldn't get the birlinns and warriors he needed to repel the Mackinnons.

She'd failed—and managed to lose her entire escort save one.

Blinking through her tears, Astrid turned her head, her gaze fastening on the hunched figure who sat nearby.

Finn looked as miserable as she felt. He'd pulled his knees under his chest and wrapped his arms around his legs.

Like her, he was shivering, although it was his face that held her attention.

She'd never seen him like this, stripped of his usual mask of arrogance.

His lean features were gaunt, and his hazel eyes glistened as he stared out of the cave entrance at the rough sea beyond.

He was grieving the crew, oblivious to her stare.

"We ... we ... n ... need to get warm," Astrid said then, her teeth chattering as she forced the words out.

Finn blinked as if coming out of a trance. His attention shifted to her, and after a heartbeat, he nodded. "I've got a flint

... but I don't think I've got the strength in me to go in search of tinder or fuel for a fire," he admitted hoarsely. "We are going to have to use our body heat to get warm."

Such an idea was horrifying, and under normal circumstances, Astrid would have snarled at him, warning him that if he laid one finger on her, she'd claw his eyes out. But these weren't normal circumstances, and she knew as well as him the shivering that now wracked them both was dangerous.

They weren't out of the woods yet, and if they didn't warm themselves up, they wouldn't survive this.

And so, Astrid nodded before pushing herself up into a sitting position.

They both still wore their heavy cloaks, although they were now soaking. Wordlessly, they stripped off their mantles, squeezing out the water as best they could—a near impossible task with fumbling, shaking hands.

Finn then yanked off his leathers, stripping down to his skin.

Astrid hesitated, mortification intruding. However, her desperate need to get warm overrode embarrassment, and she started fumbling with the laces of her surcote. "I n ... need help," she gasped.

Finn didn't answer. However, he moved close, shifting behind her so he could loosen the stays. A short while later, Astrid wore nothing but a filmy, wet lèine.

"Take that off too," Finn ordered as he attempted to wring more water out of their cloaks. "Hurry up."

Teeth gritted, Astrid obeyed. This was no time to be prudish—instead, she had to be practical. She then lay down on one of the cloaks.

An instant later, Finn had done the same and pulled the second mantle over them in a makeshift blanket.

And then his hand curved over her belly, pulling her in to spoon against him.

Astrid went rigid at the feel of his lean, hard body pressed the entire length of hers.

This whole situation was surreal. Wrong. But survival had shed them both of their inhibitions, for she was sure Finn had no desire to lie naked with her either.

The fur cloaks above and beneath them were wet, yet without her sodden, freezing clothes clinging to her skin,

Astrid's shivering eased just a little. Her teeth no longer chattered like knucklebones.

Initially, Finn's body was as cold and clammy as her own, yet as they clung together under the cloak, the chill started to thaw, and slowly but surely, their shivering drew back.

He kept his arm locked tightly around her, ensuring that their bodies were flush. She was pressed against him, all the way from her shoulders to her ankles.

It was horribly intimate, and yet she craved the contact, sinking back into him and willing warmth to soak back into her bones.

And, eventually, it did.

Finn's body seemed to warm before hers did; it was as if a furnace ignited deep inside him and slowly radiated out, cocooning her.

A sigh of relief gusted out of Astrid as she sank into his heat.

Never had any sensation been more welcome. Gradually, her shivering subsided and the sensation in her hands and feet returned. And then, her torso thawed, warmth enveloping her in a blanket.

Exhaustion hit her, the shock of what she'd just endured flattening her now that she'd reached safety and could finally relax.

Eventually, still wrapped in her enemy's arms, she drifted off to sleep.

9: BAD NEWS

FINN AWOKE TO find his face nestled in a pillow of hair. It was slightly sticky and smelled of the sea, with a faint trace of rosemary, yet it was pleasant, and as the last vestiges of sleep cleared like morning mist, he was reluctant to move away from it.

Yet he did.

Christ's bones, his mouth tasted as if he'd swallowed a pail of seawater. He desperately needed to slake his thirst.

Reaching up, he rubbed the sleep from his eyes and then propped himself up on one elbow, his gaze settling upon the naked woman who slept with her back to him.

And when it did, Finn's breathing hitched, and he momentarily forgot his dry mouth and throat. Earlier, he'd been too chilled and traumatized to pay any attention to her nudity. Yet, despite that despair sat like an anvil in his gut, it was impossible not to stare now.

Astrid's body was slender, yet the dip of her waist emphasized the swell of her hips. Lying there, as naked as the day she was born, she looked like one of the merfolk who'd ventured onto land to sleep. Her pale hair, the color of sea-foam, was tangled and wild, and her limbs were graceful, even in repose.

Finn's pulse quickened.

It was wrong to gawk at her like this, but he couldn't help himself.

Aye, he loathed Astrid, but there was no denying she was lovely. Both as delicate as apple blossom and as strong as granite. A woman full of contradictions.

Finn's groin hardened then, and he yanked himself out of his reverie.

Shifting back, he glanced down at where his rod thrust up and was now angled toward her.

God help him, he couldn't remain lying here like this. He had to move.

Heart pounding, he covered Astrid up and then scooted away, retrieving his clothing. It was devilishly uncomfortable to don, still damp and stiff with salt. It would likely chafe, but he didn't care.

He had to get dressed and leave this cave.

He needed to breathe, to regain his equilibrium. His near-drowning had shaken him up. He wasn't thinking straight.

However, he was about to flee outside when the trickling sound of water made him pause. His thirst nagged him again, providing a welcome distraction this time, and he made his way to the back of the cave, where a spring trickled through the rock. Hunkering down, he scooped the water into his mouth, taking grateful gulps until his throat no longer felt raw.

Sighing with relief, he rose to his feet once more and retraced his steps, skirting Astrid's prone figure. Ducking out of the cave, he straightened up and welcomed the sting of the wind on his face.

That was better. Suddenly, he could breathe again. The ache in his groin was subsiding too—and he wanted to forget his rod had gone into full mast over Astrid Maclean.

Thank Christ, she hadn't awoken and seen it.

Pushing the mortifying thought aside, Finn looked up. To his surprise, the sun warmed his skin and a blue sky full of scudding white clouds welcomed him.

It was as if that storm had never happened.

His stomach cramped. But it had—and he'd lost his entire crew.

Thirteen souls swept away into the deep.

His throat constricted then, his eyes stinging as he blinked back tears. No, he couldn't let himself believe it. If he and Astrid had survived, then perhaps some of the others had to. They were all able to swim—he'd deliberately only picked warriors who could.

He looked around him then, his gaze sweeping over the sandy beach below the cliffs. Maybe they'd been washed up here now too.

However, the swathe of sand was pristine, except for a large plank of wood.

The piece of the *Sea Eagle* that had saved their lives.

Inhaling the briny air deep into his lungs, Finn walked down to the plank, his boots sinking into the soft sand with each step. He then rotated in a circle, craning his neck as he gazed up at the cliffs.

He had no idea where he was. It was likely one of the Small Isles, yet he didn't know which. The first thing he had to do was look for help. Surely, there would be a village nearby where they could find food and shelter?

First though, he returned to the cave with heavy steps, checking on Astrid.

The lass still slept, huddled under the fur cloak like a hibernating squirrel. He didn't want to disturb her, and it looked as if she'd sleep a little longer.

Finn gazed at her a long moment, even as despair continued to press its heavy hands upon his shoulders. What a mess they were in; he didn't know how they'd manage to reach Skye in time to help Loch now.

With a heavy sigh, Finn turned and left the cave once more.

Astrid yawned and stretched, a feeling of wellbeing suffusing her.

However, when she opened her eyes, that sensation fled.

She was alone, in a dank cave, naked save for the fur cloak that covered her modesty.

Pulse lurching into a gallop, she sat up, clutching the cloak to her chest. Her memories of what had happened after they'd washed up on the shore were blurry—she remembered little more than cold and desperation—although she *did* recall that she and Finn had slept naked, curled up together.

Hot and then cold washed over her.

Where was he now?

Heart still hammering, she rolled to her feet and reached for her clothing. Perhaps he'd needed to relieve himself. It was best she made use of the privacy while she still had it.

Fumbling in haste, Astrid yanked on her lèine and kirtle. Wriggling into her surcote was a little harder, although at least her fingers obeyed her now. It took some work, but eventually, she managed to lace the back. It was a messy job, but she didn't care. She even strapped on her weapons, for having her blades close settled the anxiety that now tightened her chest. Pulling on her damp hose and boots, she then moved to the back of the cave, where water trickled down the damp stone.

Hesitating only a moment, for her mouth felt like a dry strip of leather, she cupped her hands under it and drank. It was a little brackish, yet she knew the taste of spring water.

Slaking her thirst, Astrid then left the cave, emerging blinking into the sunlight.

Finn was nowhere to be seen.

Usually, such a realization would have pleased her. Not so now. There was only the two of them, stranded on a beach in the middle of nowhere.

Astrid's breathing grew shallow then. The bastard hadn't run off and left her, had he?

Trying not to panic, she made her way down onto the beach. Ironically, it was a lovely morning—it seemed they'd slept the afternoon and the night away—and the sea was calm.

An ache rose under her ribs then, twisting hard as she thought about the crew. Steadfast Colin, protective Roy, earnest Dougie, and cheeky Norris—and the others who'd embarked on this journey with them. All brave, loyal men.

Astrid clasped her hands together, her eyes closing as she lifted her face to the sky. She always turned to God when times were tough. Duart Castle's chapel had been her sanctuary during many trials. Indeed, after Maggie's death, and the passing of her parents, she'd knelt at a pew in the echoey silence, seeking solace from the pain that split her asunder. And when Loch had promised her to Kendric Mackinnon, she'd disappeared in the chapel for hours at a time, hoping that prayer might change his mind.

It hadn't—only her illness and reading the missive their father had left him had done that.

But Astrid hadn't given up on prayer, and now she whispered to God to keep their crew members safe. She had to believe that if she and Finn had found safety, some of the others had too.

"Astrid!"

A man's voice intruded then, and she twisted right to see a lean figure, dressed in salt-encrusted leathers, trudging up the beach toward her.

Finn carried a load of sticks under one arm although his expression was grim.

Astrid stiffened at the sight of him, as she always did. She couldn't help it. Now that her life wasn't in imminent danger, she was herself again.

And judging from the coldness in Finn's eyes as he viewed her, so was he.

"Bad news," he said curtly, reaching Astrid and drawing to a halt.

Her mouth pursed. "What? Other than we're shipwrecked, and the rest of our party have likely drowned?"

He nodded, his expression unchanging. "I've just taken a walk around this isle ... it's a tiny rock with nothing but gannets and puffins living here."

A chill washed over Astrid. "No," she breathed.

"Aye."

"Where are we?"

"There are a few uninhabited isles on the western edge of the Small Isles; I'd say we've washed up on one of them."

Panic slammed into Astrid, grasping her by the throat.

God's holy rood, they were doomed.

"What are we going to do?" she whispered, cursing the way her voice wobbled.

Finn's lips thinned before he nodded at the armload of driftwood and clumps of dry grass he carried. "I'm going to see about building us a fire," he said curtly. "Then I'll go out again and try and steal some puffin eggs."

"I wasn't talking about that," she snapped. "What are we going to do about the fact we're marooned on a deserted rock?"

Finn flashed her a humorless smile. "Ye were praying earlier ... ye might as well return to it." He brushed past her then, heading toward the cave. "Looks like that's the only thing that'll help us now."

10: THE TRUTH ISN'T PRETTY

THE PUFFIN EGG was salty and slightly fishy—but Astrid wolfed it down fast.

Finn had fried the egg on a large flat stone he'd carried into the mouth of the cave and set amongst the embers. He'd used a thin shard of stone to flip the egg onto a smaller rock he'd collected, which they were using as a makeshift trencher. In his foraging, he'd managed to collect four eggs. They were larger than those from a fowl, and although the meal wouldn't fill their bellies, it would take the edge off their hunger for a bit.

Astrid watched as Finn fried the second egg and flipped it onto the stone. She'd thought he'd eat that one, but, to her surprise, he handed it over to her.

Remembering her manners, Astrid took it with a nod.

They'd spoken little since Finn had returned with the precious eggs nestled in the crook of his arm. He'd been away a while, and in the meantime, Astrid had walked farther down the beach, collecting more driftwood.

She'd also discovered that Finn hadn't been exaggerating. This isle was tiny. It would take less than an hour to walk its perimeter. As she'd collected wood for the fire, Astrid kept glancing out to sea, hoping to see a passing birlinn or merchant's cog. But the flat blue surface was unblemished this morning.

Returning to the cave, she'd added her wood to the pile and waited.

Around noon, Finn had reappeared with the eggs. He'd then produced a flint from a pouch upon his belt and used a handful of dry grass and twigs as tinder to get a fire started.

And all the while, Astrid silently looked on. Her mood was as somber as her companion's face. Neither of them had anything to say to each other, and the silence suited her well.

Finishing her second egg now, she watched as Finn cooked his own meal before devouring his eggs within moments.

He then glanced up, meeting her eye squarely for the first time in hours. "We won't have an endless supply of puffin eggs," he pointed out, his voice slightly surly, as if he resented having to address her. "I'll see if I can fashion a slingshot and get us a puffin or gannet ... but we'll need other sources of food too."

"I take it ye're capable of spearfishing?"

His mouth compressed. "Good enough." He glanced over at the pile of firewood. "Maybe I can sharpen a point from one of those."

Astrid's belly tightened as the full reality of their predicament settled over her.

They were stranded, and no one knew they were here. Nothing grew on this isle, and they risked exhausting their supplies.

Her breathing became shallow then. Until yesterday, a dull fear lurked in the marrow of her bones about what might happen if Kendric Mackinnon bested her brother at Dounarwyse. Would the 'Butcher of Dùn Ara' lay siege to Duart then too, pressing his advantage?

But now it was difficult to worry about anything but the fact she was stranded on this rock. She imagined the future then. What would become of them if no one found them here?

Astrid shuddered and wrapped her arms about herself.

Marking her reaction, Finn frowned. "Best not to think about what lies ahead," he said tersely. "It'll only drive ye mad."

"I can't help it," she gasped out the words. "There's a very real possibility we'll die here."

Curse her, she needed to be strong now. She couldn't crumble. Not yet.

His mouth twisted into a humorless smile. "Aye ... what an irony, eh? To think that the last person each of us will see will be our enemy."

Astrid stiffened. Her mouth pursed then. "Aye ... maybe this is God's punishment," she replied. "Wrath is one of the seven deadly sins, after all."

Across the fire, Finn stilled. A moment later, his gaze narrowed. "Aye," he said quietly. "Although I won't give my anger up."

Astrid stared back at him before heat flared in her stomach, melting the fear and dread that had frozen there. "Neither will I."

"Well, it looks as if there's something ye and I finally agree on."

Astrid drew herself up. The sneer in his voice made her lust for blood. Leaning forward, she listened to the quick thud of her heart. "My only regret is that the laird saved yer neck that day," she said slowly, her voice vibrating with anger. "Ye deserved to be strung up at those crossroads for what ye did."

Finn leaned in, mirroring her gesture. "I didn't kill Maggie," he said, enunciating each word carefully. "I swore it before ye all."

Astrid's mouth twisted. "Yer story was weak. Ye stole a rowboat and took Maggie out. She went swimming and then got into trouble and drowned." Rage now drummed like rain on rock inside her. "But Maggie was an able swimmer. She wouldn't have gotten into difficulty. What really happened is that ye took liberties, and she rebuffed ye ... and in a fit of temper, ye drowned her."

Finn's hazel eyes glinted dangerously. "No."

"Did things play out a little differently?" she demanded, deliberately goading him now. "Did she try to swim back to shore, and in yer zeal to stop her, ye accidentally pushed her under the water?" Astrid's throat tightened then, her voice catching on those last words. Lord, it was hard to talk about Maggie. Even now, years on, the thought of her friend's terror in those last moments twisted her up inside. How she wished her friend hadn't stepped onto that boat with Finn.

"No."

He straightened up, a nerve ticking under one eye. Finn's features had hardened, and his gaze was flinty. His hands had balled into fists now; he was having trouble leashing his temper. "Ye couldn't stomach the truth, Astrid," he growled. "It would shatter the rosy memories ye have of yer friend."

"Excuse me?"

"Ye saw just one side to Maggie Garvie ... but she had another, darker, face, and she—"

"Dog!" Astrid leaped to her feet, cutting him off. "How dare ye insult the dead?"

He stared up at her. "I'm not," he ground out. "I'm telling ye what happened."

Astrid started to tremble then, such was the force of the fury churning inside her. "So, Maggie revealed herself as less than perfect, did she?" she snarled. "And ye killed her for it?"

Finn lurched to his feet. "No!" He then stepped around the fire and strode toward her. "Curse it, woman … still yer tongue and listen!"

Astrid jerked back as if he'd just slapped her. She'd never seen Finn lose his temper before, and fear speared her when she witnessed the fury in his eyes. Backing up, she tried to escape him, but he kept coming, and moments later, her spine hit the damp wall of the cave.

Finn stepped in close, placing a hand on either side of her head to cage her in.

Astrid reached up and shoved at his chest, yet he didn't move. "Get away from me!" she gasped. Her voice rose in pitch, revealing that she was on the edge of panic. Deep down, she'd craved this confrontation for years, but now that it was happening, she was desperate to get away.

It wasn't playing out as she'd imagined.

Finn's proximity overwhelmed her senses and made her feel out of control.

Coward! a voice screamed in her head. *It's easy to be brave at a distance … but where is yer courage when ye truly need it?*

"I'll keep my distance all right," Finn countered, each word hard and clipped. "But not until I tell ye what really happened that day … the tale I've told only the old laird. Not even Loch or Jack have heard it."

"Why keep it to yerself?" Lifting her chin, Astrid glared up at him, even as her heart quailed. This close, she could see the flecks of green and dark brown in her adversary's eyes. She could taste his banked rage.

"Because the truth isn't pretty."

Astrid's blood started to roar in her ears. She didn't understand where he was going with this, yet she didn't want to hear it. She wasn't going to let him speak ill of her best friend, the kindest soul that Astrid had ever met.

Long moments passed, and when Finn continued, there was a rasp to his voice. "The truth is that it was never Maggie I wanted ... it was *ye*."

Astrid froze, her lips parting. Of all the things she thought he might say, this wasn't one of them.

Marking her response, Finn's mouth twisted. "Aye, fear not, my infatuation ended the day ye sent the grief-maddened fishermen of Craignure after me ... but before that, I pined for the laird's aloof flaxen-haired daughter. I never said a word to Loch and Jack about it ... for I knew they'd ridicule me, but in secret, my need for ye grew." He paused then, his gaze narrowing. "It was hopeless though, for ye barely noticed I lived and breathed."

Astrid's chest started to ache, and she realized she'd stopped breathing. Heaving in a lungful of air, she flattened herself hard against the wall, her clenched fists still pressing against his ribs.

But still, Finn didn't budge. "And then yer friend made her interest in me clear," he continued, his voice flattening now. "Maggie was sweet, but it wasn't *her* I wanted. Nonetheless, I flirted with the lass in front of ye ... foolishly believing it might make ye jealous." He gave a soft snort then as if he couldn't believe his own idiocy. "That was a mistake ... for she fastened herself to me like a burr. Soon, wherever I went, there she was."

Astrid closed her eyes, squeezing them shut. She willed him to stop talking, to cease his tale now, but it was futile. Now that Finn had begun talking, it was as if a tide had been released. The words flooded forth, and there was no stopping them.

"The months passed ... and then, one eve in high summer, Maggie asked me to take her out on the Sound." Finn let out a slow breath, as if steeling himself to continue, before pushing on. "I wasn't interested ... but when I told her I wouldn't go, she started weeping ... and then, when it was clear her tears weren't having the desired effect, she threatened me."

Astrid's eyes snapped open. "*Threatened* ye?" His story had turned nonsensical. "What? Did she say she'd blacken yer eye if ye didn't do as she asked?" The idea was ridiculous. Maggie had been small and birdlike, and although leanly built, Finn was far more intimidating.

"No," Finn growled, anger sparking in his gaze once more. "She threatened to go to the laird and tell him that I'd raped her."

Astrid's breathing caught, dizziness sweeping over her. "Liar!"

She smacked her fists into his chest once more, yet Finn shook his head, denying her outburst.

A muscle flexed in his jaw as he continued. "I was angry, yet there was a glint, a desperation, in Maggie's eyes that told me she'd do as she threatened." Finn paused then, his features tightening. "I knew I wasn't popular locally ... the wild lad from Islay who thought rules were for other folk. I drank, brawled, and led Loch and Jack into a lot of situations that landed us all in hot water. I'd already gotten in trouble with the laird a few times, and he had me on a final warning. One more transgression and he'd send me back to Dunnyveg in disgrace. I couldn't risk it." He drew in a deep breath then before releasing it slowly. "And so, against my better judgment, I let her blackmail me."

11: OUTRAGEOUS LIES

HOW THE DEVIL had this happened?

Finn had told himself that he'd never reveal the truth of what happened between him and Maggie Garvie to anyone save Iain Maclean. The old laird of Duart had taken his secret to the grave with him, and that had been a relief.

But now he was recounting the whole sordid affair—to Astrid of all people.

The last person he'd ever intended to confide it.

And to make matters worse, he'd gone and told her that he'd once pined for her.

Aye, she'd provoked him. With her scornful gaze and haughty voice, treating him as if he were a turd she'd just scraped off her boot. Finally, her baiting had gotten too much.

Astrid wouldn't like the truth, yet she'd hear it. Every last vile word of it.

Nonetheless, telling her how he'd secretly longed for her all those years ago had cost him. He'd done his best to forget about that infatuation, especially since Astrid was now the last woman he wanted. But it was part of the tale, and so he recounted it.

He'd heard it said that when someone released a burden they felt better—and the truth about Maggie's death that he'd been carrying all these years was a weight indeed. However, speaking of what had happened between him and the lass didn't bring any relief. It just made him feel queasy. Guilty.

"Maggie didn't have a boat for us ... so she dared me to steal one," he continued then, his gaze never leaving Astrid's face. She was staring up at him, her delicate features rigid, her dark eyes blazing—but Finn stayed where he was, pinning her between the cage of his arms.

The shrew would hear him out.

"I took a fisherman's rowboat from near Craignure and rowed us out. It was a bonnie evening although a stiff breeze made the water rough." Finn halted then, steeling himself for the words he'd have to utter next. "When we were a distance from shore, Maggie revealed the real reason she'd asked me to take her out on the Sound. She wanted me to row us to a sheltered cove ... she wanted me to lie with her."

Astrid made a choking sound, indicating that she felt this claim as ludicrous and appalling as his last. Finn's gut clenched. This was why he'd kept the truth a secret all this time. It sounded as if he'd woven an elaborate falsehood, painting a vulnerable young woman as a schemer to save his own neck.

And Maggie wasn't here to tell her side of the tale either.

Finn had wept with relief when Iain Maclean had believed him that afternoon they'd sat alone together in the clan-chief's solar. He'd been sure the laird would call him a liar, but he hadn't.

"I said 'no'," he continued, his voice lowering now. "Don't get me wrong, I was a red-blooded lad, and usually a lass offering to lift her skirts was all I dreamed about ... but Maggie's manipulation had already vexed me. Instinctively, I sensed she was trying to trap me. If I lay with her, she could end up with bairn and use that to force me to wed her." Finn cleared his throat. "She starting weeping then ... and when I didn't soften, she tried threatening me again. But I still didn't relent. Instead, I turned the boat around for shore ... and she flew into a rage, clawing at my face. Realizing that she'd taken things too far, she then grew desperate."

Finn halted there, his throat suddenly tight. The queasiness that had crept upon him as he'd begun this story was increasing now. God's troth, it had been a nasty business, and, his lingering guilt aside, the memory of it had tainted his view of women ever since.

Meanwhile, Astrid's breathing had turned shallow and fast. Her face was now the color of milk. She looked close to fainting.

Finn's chest constricted. Astrid was ferociously clever and could be a spitting hellcat at times, yet she wasn't as formidable as she appeared. Her response to the betrothal Loch had organized to Kendric Mackinnon had proved that she was more sensitive than most folk realized. Once it had become clear her brother wouldn't relent, she slipped into a dangerous melancholy, one that had made her sicken and waste away.

Aye, he wanted her to know the truth, yet he didn't wish to traumatize her. Nonetheless, he still hadn't finished his tale. Not yet.

"Maggie declared that if I didn't do her bidding, she'd take her own life," he admitted hoarsely. "I told her I didn't believe her ... and that's when she threw herself overboard."

Astrid's eyes brimmed with tears then, and they trickled down her cheeks. "No," she whispered, a quaver in her voice.

"Aye," he replied softly. "And ye are right ... she was a strong swimmer. I dove in after her, yet she outdistanced me quickly ... and swam east, away from the coast toward the heart of the Sound. The waves grew choppier, and I risked getting into trouble ... and then, up ahead, I saw Maggie disappear under the water." He halted, swallowing. "She cried out, right before she disappeared ... for help. I swam out to where she vanished ... and even dove as far as I could to look for her ... but it was as if a strong current had caught her and dragged her away."

Finn stopped talking then as remorse gripped his chest in a vise. Astrid knew the rest. How he'd returned to Craignure distraught, and how all the fishermen there including Maggie's father had started searching for her. They didn't find the lass though, and the tide brought her body to shore the following day.

Silence fell in the cave then, one that shivered with tension.

Finn had done it—he'd told Astrid the truth. Nonetheless, her strained face and haunted gaze revealed that she didn't believe him. He wasn't surprised. His story didn't suit the idea of him she'd clung to over the years.

An idea he hadn't gone to the trouble of changing.

To her, he was ruthless, cynical, and self-centered—a man not to be trusted. And perhaps all those things were right. Finn was no saint; he knew it. His parents had too, which was why they'd packed him off all those years earlier.

But he wasn't a murderer.

Astrid appeared to have sunk into a trance following the conclusion of his tale. Her gaze turned inward, as if she'd just traveled back to the past and was reliving Maggie's final days.

He wondered if anything he'd said had made her view things differently.

Eventually though, she roused herself, blinking. Her fists still rested upon his chest, and despite himself, Finn found something reassuring about the contact. Holding her within the cage of his arms was dominant, although he'd been careful not to touch her.

Astrid's peat-brown eyes glistened, grief rippling across her face. Her throat then bobbed. She pressed against his ribs with her knuckles once more, making it clear that she wanted him to step back.

And this time, he obeyed.

He braced himself for her scorn then, for the sharp edge of her tongue that he'd come to know so well over the years.

But she didn't speak.

Instead, casting him a look that would have made a weaker man quail, she pushed herself off the damp rock wall and stumbled past him, heading for the cave mouth.

Finn let her go without a word.

As soon as she was free of the cave, and Finn's presence, the tears that Astrid had been struggling to hold back blinded her.

She staggered down the dune outside and onto the beach. She had to get as far as possible from the devil. Scrubbing at her cheeks, she glanced over her shoulder, almost as if she expected Finn to come after her.

But he didn't.

Still, she hurried on, although it was slow going through the soft sand. The tide had risen, covering the coarser, hard-packed sand and leaving the fine, powdery stuff to trudge through.

Astrid pushed on, panting as sobs clawed their way up her throat.

Lies. Disgusting, outrageous lies.

He'd poured them over her, forced her to listen to them. How she wished she could have blocked her ears, for even though his tale was an utter fabrication, there was no unhearing it.

He'd painted her dear friend as a manipulative, unstable, and desperate young woman.

She wouldn't believe such rot.

And yet Finn's face had been strained as he told the story. He'd dropped his usual calculating look. His eyes had been stormy, deeply shadowed, and his voice rough. Aye, it hadn't been easy for him. But then, spinning such deceit wouldn't be easy.

How long had it taken him to come up with such a far-fetched tale? And why tell her now? They were stranded here, their futures uncertain indeed. Was this his way of getting even with her finally, for the part she'd played in whipping the locals up into a frenzy? Did he want to ensure he didn't go to his grave without having his revenge?

Astrid wrapped her arms around herself. The wind was brisk and not overly cold, yet she felt chilled to the bone. She'd left her cloak in the cave and wouldn't be going back for it.

Reaching the end of the long strand, she climbed onto the rocky point, near where the puffins nested. The isle ended here—there was nothing but sea beyond.

Out of breath, Astrid slumped down on the rock and looked out across the water. It was getting late in the day now, although the sun wouldn't set behind her for a while yet. The light had turned golden, gleaming over the glossy sea.

Staring out at the horizon, she tried not to think about the things Finn had told her. Instead, she focused on the crew members they'd lost the day before. She'd prayed that some of them might have been washed up on this isle too, but there had been no sign of them.

All she could hope was that they'd been carried farther east, onto one of the larger isles, or that a passing ship had picked them up.

She couldn't, wouldn't, believe they were all gone.

And neither would she believe Finn's slanderous tale about her best friend.

Astrid's belly twisted then, her breathing growing fast and shallow. She was out of her depth now—as she'd been when it had become clear Loch would indeed force her to wed Kendric Mackinnon.

It was all too much.

She could feel the darkness clawing at her, could feel reality drawing back. It would be so easy to give in to it, to let despair take her—to sink into oblivion as she had six months earlier.

Sweating now, Astrid balled her hands into fists and pressed them hard against the rock.

No, she had to fight this *weakness*.

12: A SEED OF DOUBT

PULLING HER KNEES up, Astrid wrapped her arms around her shins, hugging tightly. She placed her forehead on her knees and squeezed her eyes shut. She then concentrated on slowing and deepening her breathing.

Her cheeks were still wet with tears, yet she managed to keep her despair at bay—just.

Time drew out, and once she'd regained control, Astrid finally allowed herself to dwell on Finn's shocking revelations.

She recalled the scratches on his face after the incident. At the time, it had just incriminated him further, for it looked as if there had been a struggle between him and Maggie.

But Finn had told her that Maggie attacked him.

Astrid couldn't imagine Maggie clawing at anyone's face. It made no sense.

Drawing in a deep breath, she cast her mind back then, traveling to when she'd been fifteen summers old and as thick as thieves with the fisherman's daughter. Had Maggie ever lost her temper with Astrid?

Only once.

It had been Bealtunn, just a few weeks before the fateful day they'd met Loch, Jack, and Finn on the way back from Craignure. Maggie had been excited for the festival, which marked the first day of summer. It was an eve when couples often declared their interest in each other, and when some would go 'green gowning'—sneaking off into the shadows to lie together. Many marriages took place shortly after Bealtunn. And, indeed, it was also why so many bairns were born around Yuletide.

Maggie had started showing a lot of interest in lads at that time. Whereas Astrid was still content to ride her pony and explore the coastline around Duart, her friend was changing. Maggie had taken to talking about the lads she liked and the ones she wished would notice her. And she'd often suggest their walks took them by the men-at-arms at Duart, who were training outdoors, or the young men who worked the fields. This change in her friend had irritated Astrid. She wasn't interested in flirting and was cowed by the lewd comments and catcalls that followed them when they got too close to men.

This Bealtunn, Maggie wasn't as enthralled by the dancing as she'd usually been or interested in sneaking cups of mulled cider and playing pranks on other lasses. Instead, she'd stared at the lads who'd attended the celebration, including Loch.

Even at barely twenty, Astrid's brother carried himself with a reckless arrogance that made the lasses swarm around him.

Maggie's stares had gotten so obvious that, eventually, Astrid had told her to stop. It was embarrassing her.

And to her shock, her sweet friend had turned nasty. "Ye don't think I'm worthy of him, is that it?" Maggie had snarled.

"N ... no, of c ... course not," Astrid had stammered, taken aback by her vicious response. "But Loch's a rogue when it comes to the lasses ... and I wouldn't want ye to get hurt." That was true, although the thought of her brother and her friend flirting was disconcerting, to say the least.

Maggie's blue eyes had narrowed, her anger simmering. "I don't need ye to look out for me, Astrid," she'd said then. "Let me choose whether a man is right for me or not."

A wave of heat washed over Astrid then as she recalled the incident. It had been short, yet she'd marked her friend's words and afterward had been wary of commenting on the lads Maggie showed an interest in.

So, when Maggie had thrown herself at Finn, she'd held her tongue.

And now that Astrid had recalled that incident, she remembered other details—things that she viewed in a new light. Maggie's brittle good humor at times, as if she was hiding something. Her unhappy life at home, for her parents fought like pit dogs and drew her into their squabbles. Maggie had been desperate to leave home, yet unless she found a husband, she couldn't. Astrid remembered her friend's growing obsession with lads, to the point where she talked about nothing else.

Maybe Finn isn't lying, a voice whispered to her. *Maybe.*

Astrid scrunched her eyes tight. "No!" she gasped. She wouldn't believe it. If he was right, then Maggie's death was even more tragic. It would mean that her beloved Maggie was unstable and suffering, and yet had said nothing to her best friend.

It would mean that Astrid hadn't really known her at all.

It was dark by the time Astrid returned to the cave.

As she'd expected, Finn was still awake. He sat cross-legged by the faintly glowing hearth, wrapping a thin strip of leather around a fork-shaped piece of driftwood. At the scuff of her boot, his chin kicked up and their gazes met.

"I was about to go looking for ye," he greeted her gruffly.

Astrid gave a soft snort. "I couldn't go far, could I?"

"No," he replied. "But ye were upset when ye left. I thought ye might have gone and done something ... foolish."

Astrid's step faltered at these words, and she drew to a halt a couple of yards from the fire. "Like Maggie?" she whispered.

Cold washed over her then. Of course, Finn had witnessed her humiliating 'illness' over her betrothal to Mackinnon. He likely thought her weak and volatile. Did everyone at Duart see her that way now?

However, there was no disdain on Finn's face as he stared back at her. Instead, his gaze guttered before he looked away.

Astrid watched him, her brow furrowing. She'd spent hours going over the things he'd said, and then sorting through her memories of Maggie. She still didn't believe him, but the bastard had planted a seed of doubt in her mind, one that had now germinated and was steadily growing.

All the same, part of her wanted to rail at him, to tell him he was not just a murderer, but an arch-manipulator. Yet she held her tongue. She was exhausted, body and soul, too tired to fight any longer.

Swallowing the ire that merely the sight of him roused, she lowered herself to the ground opposite the dying hearth. "Ye're letting the fire go out."

"Aye ... best I save our fuel for cooking. It's not cold."

No, it wasn't, although Astrid found herself shivering all the same. It was likely a culmination of tiredness and shock, but she felt as if she'd never be warm again. Picking up the cloak she'd left behind, she slung it over her shoulders and wrapped it tightly around herself.

Her eyes were scratchy from weeping and exhaustion. Her body ached, while her belly was hollow. The two puffin eggs she'd eaten earlier were a distant memory. Her stomach gave a loud growl then, and Astrid winced, placing her hand upon it.

Glancing over at Finn, she noted that he was observing her, his expression veiled now. "I'm making a slingshot" —he nodded to the item in his hands— "I'll go hunting tomorrow."

Astrid nodded.

His jaw tightened then. "I'll do my best to make sure ye don't starve."

Astrid's eyes widened. His words took her aback. The man loathed her, yet ever since the storm, he'd taken care of her, looked out for her with an attentiveness that contradicted the hostility she'd witnessed in his gaze all these years.

Ye are Loch's sister, she reminded herself then. *And he'd do anything for his friend.* Indeed, Loch and Jack were the only two people alive that Finn seemed to care about.

He cared about ye once too.

Astrid's jaw tightened at this reminder. Maybe, but those days were long gone.

Indeed, Finn was a lone wolf. She'd never heard him mention his family back on Islay—and she'd never witnessed him show any warmth or affection toward a woman.

In fact, since his return to Mull, she had barely seen him interact with lasses, besides her and Mairi, at all. Had Maggie's death scarred him so badly?

Astrid caught herself. Aye, of course, it had. It had scarred them *all*. Even murderers could develop a conscience with the passing of the years.

However, even as she reassured herself, the voice that had whispered to her earlier returned. *If he's telling the truth, it would be difficult to trust any woman again.*

Astrid ground her teeth. Enough of this nonsense. She wasn't about to let compassion for Finn in—she wouldn't allow exhaustion and despair to muddle her tangled thoughts any further.

It was time she got some much-needed rest.

Without another word, Astrid stretched out on the hard floor, rolling onto her side and giving him her back.

She'd thought it would take her a while to get to sleep, for the stone floor of the cave was hard and uncomfortable. Yet she underestimated just how drained she was. The moment Astrid nestled her head into the crook of her arm, fatigue crashed into her.

And a heartbeat or two after that, sleep pulled her under.

Finn awoke to find himself alone in the cave.

Sitting up, he blinked and tried to get his bearings. The sun rose early this time of year, yet the light that filtered into the cave mouth was still dim.

Where was Astrid?

Rolling to his feet, Finn shrugged off his cloak and headed outside. And as he went, apprehension knotted his gut.

Yesterday, he'd been reminded of Astrid's fragility, and in the long hours until she returned to the cave, he'd considered what effect the truth might have on her. He'd let his temper best him earlier. If he'd been thinking clearly, he'd never have told her what really happened to Maggie.

He'd felt vindicated initially, seeking to punish Astrid, but as he recounted the tale, he'd regretted taking this course.

It didn't change anything.

Maggie was still dead. Many of the fisherfolk of Craignure still blamed him for her death—as did Astrid.

But when she'd fled from the cave, he'd worried what she might do.

His first instinct had been to follow her, yet he'd quashed it. She wouldn't welcome his presence, and he had to trust that she wouldn't let grief and anger make her lose her wits.

All the same, he'd been relieved when she'd returned to the cave.

Finn had sensed a change in her too. It was clear she still didn't believe him. However, she'd lost her rage. Like him, she'd spent their time apart thinking things over.

There was an uneasy truce between them now. That came as a relief to Finn, for they had enough to worry about at present, without being at each other's throats all the time.

No, he shouldn't have worried that Astrid would do something rash—for he spotted her then.

It was low tide, and the lass had kicked off her boots, knotted her skirts around her thighs, and walked out as far as she could to where the water glittered in the distance.

She was now crouched over, digging into the wet sand with a knife.

Intrigued, Finn drew near.

It was another bonnie morning, and the early sun had turned the calm sea molten gold. The sun also gilded Astrid, making her pale hair gleam, and bringing out the glow in her creamy skin.

Finn's gait slowed as he approached her, and without meaning to, he took the sight of her in—silently admiring her slender, yet shapely, legs. There was no doubt about it, Astrid Maclean was lovely. He remembered then, how just the sight of her years ago was enough to make his chest ache. How he'd stolen glances at her whenever he could.

Finn's mouth thinned. What a fool he'd been. Looks were deceiving—and he'd learned that the hard way.

Astrid glanced up, her eyes snapping wide as she spied his approach. "Stop!" she cried out, whipping the long-bladed knife out of the sand and waving it at him. "Don't come any closer."

13: DIGGING UP SPOOTS

FINN CAME TO an abrupt halt, his brow furrowing. "What are ye doing?"

Astrid gestured to the sling she'd created with her skirts, which was rapidly filling with thin, tube-shaped shellfish. "Digging up spoots ... and ye are about to chase them away!"

The glint in her eyes, and the delight she was trying hard to throttle, made Finn's breathing catch.

He'd never seen Astrid like this. As the laird's daughter, she had an important role, yet there was a cloak of aloofness and dignity that she always maintained. But out here, on this empty rock in the middle of the sea, with only him as a witness, she had not a care about tying up her skirts and collecting shellfish like a fisherman's wife.

And for the first time in a long while, Finn caught a glimpse of the lass he'd once longed for.

Trying to ignore the strange tug in his chest, he raised an eyebrow. "*How* exactly do I risk chasing them away?"

"See those little spouts of water shooting out of the sand?" She gestured with the wicked knife she grasped. Its blade glinted in the sunlight, and Finn recognized it as a throwing knife, one that she'd drawn from the belt about her hips. "That's the spoots fleeing." Her mouth quirked. "They can feel yer footsteps approaching ... the trick is to sneak up on them."

Finn folded his arms across his chest. "With a knife?"

"Aye ... like this."

She leaped forward then, nimble as a sprite, and plunged the throwing knife into the coarse, wet sand where water had just jetted to the surface. She then plunged her fingers down next to the blade.

A moment later, she plucked a long tubular shell out, holding it aloft. "Ye cut into the sand and then push the knife alongside the shell to stop the spoot from fleeing ... it makes it easier to root them out."

Finn couldn't help it; he smiled. "It looks like ye have quite a few already," he noted, impressed.

"Aye ... I need to collect as many as I can before the tide turns." She paused then, glancing over her shoulder at the glinting water in the distance. "I'm so hungry, I could eat a mountain of these."

Finn's stomach rumbled in agreement. He inclined his head then. "How does a clan-chief's daughter learn to gather spoots?"

Her gaze fused with his. "Maggie taught me," she replied, her tone cooling. "She was a fisherman's daughter, after all."

An awkward silence fell then before Finn cleared his throat. After their exchange the night before, he was wary of responding to any comments about Maggie. "Right." He heeled off his boots and rolled up his braies. He then drew his dirk. "I'd better help ye."

Astrid cast him a wary look as if she expected there to be a jibe underneath the offer.

However, for once, there wasn't.

"Put yer dirk away," she said after a pause before drawing a blade from her belt and holding it out to him. "These work better."

Finn nodded, resheathing his dirk and taking the knife from her. "Very well," he said, inclining his head. "Give me another demonstration of how it's done."

Astrid's dark eyes glinted once more, and then she took a few slow steps backward, casting her gaze over the wet sand. Moments later, spying a jet of water, she danced sideways, sliced her knife through the sand, and then extracted another shell with her free hand. "Go on," she said, a challenge in her voice now. "Let's see if ye have any luck ... I suggest ye walk backward though, as I just did, so ye can see them 'spoot' ... and move *slowly*."

Finn nodded. He wasn't one to shy away from a challenge, and fortunately, he was light on his feet. He was grateful for the distraction too—collecting skittish shellfish was easier than dwelling on their predicament.

Even so, catching spoots wasn't as easy as Astrid made it look—and it took him several attempts before he grabbed his first one.

Straightening up, Finn threw his catch to Astrid. "See that?"

However, Astrid merely cast him a wry look as she deposited the spoot in the bag she'd made with her skirts. "Aye … although could ye hurry yerself up? At this rate, ye'll catch three by the time the tide comes in."

Taking her point, Finn got back to work. And once he got the knack of it, he did speed up.

They both retreated into silence, working to collect more shellfish. And as he surveyed the wet sand for the tell-tale spouts of water, Finn's thoughts kept straying to their situation. He wasn't a man who let fate dictate his path through life, but right now, he'd never felt so helpless.

There was literally no way off this isle.

There was also nothing here to attract visitors.

They were at Fortuna's mercy now, and Finn hated it. His mind scrabbled, exploring every avenue, yet he always arrived back at the same place. Stuck.

"If yer scowl gets any deeper, the spoots will bury themselves even farther into the sand in fright." Astrid's rueful voice intruded then, and Finn's chin kicked up.

His gaze met his companion's, and he pulled a face. "I hate feeling this powerless," he admitted roughly. "I'm used to being able to take action when things go awry … but all I can do is wait."

Astrid's delicate features tightened, her gaze shadowing as she nodded. "Aye," she agreed softly. "Loch will be battling the Mackinnons now, and I'm supposed to bring him help." Her shoulders sagged then. "He was relying on me, and I've failed him."

Finn's gut clenched at the thought of what was unfolding at Dounarwyse. "We *both* have."

Once they'd caught enough spoots, Astrid and Finn walked back across the tidal flats toward the beach. It was a warm morning, so Finn brought a stack of wood down from the cave and built a fire on the sand above the tideline.

There, they cooked the spoots upon a bed of embers, watching as each one popped open to reveal the long thin strip of meat within. They then used sticks to lift the tubular shells from the fire.

Finn yelped in pain as he burned his fingers.

"Here." Astrid drew one of her throwing knives from the belt about her waist and passed it to him. "This should make it easier."

Sucking his injured fingertips, Finn nodded his thanks. Meanwhile, Astrid pulled out another of her precious knives and plucked the flesh from the shell she'd removed from the fire. She then popped the shellfish in her mouth, stifling a sigh of pleasure. The spoots were a little gritty, as they hadn't soaked them in fresh water first, but the meat was both sweet and tangy, and she was *starving*.

"These do the trick nicely ... useful for catching spoots *and* eating them." Finn held up the throwing knife, its thin blade glinting in the sun. Like her, the juice ran down his chin, yet he paid it no mind. "Although I can't get used to seeing ye bearing weapons."

Astrid pulled a face. "Ye're no better than Loch." She ate another mouthful of spoots before continuing, "While ye were all away chasing after the English, I learned how to defend myself with a blade ... how to fight."

Finn's mouth pursed. "Aye, ye are a menace with a knife."

Astrid stilled. Of course, he was referring to that incident last year when she'd thrown an eating knife at him in Loch's solar. It had embedded into the wall, just inches from his head. "I deliberately missed that day," she replied after a pause. It was the truth. Her aim was good enough that she could have killed him.

Finn scowled. "And why is that? Ye had yer chance to rid yerself of me ... yet ye didn't take it."

Their gazes fused, and Astrid considered his question for a few moments before she answered, "I'm not a murderer."

Not like ye.

Finn stiffened. She hadn't said the words, although they hung in the air between them all the same.

They resumed their meal then, silence settling between them. However, the fragile rapport that had developed while they collected and cooked the spoots was now gone. Their conversation had reminded them both of their feud and the reasons they couldn't stand each other.

Aye, Astrid had focused on filling their bellies this morning, but she hadn't forgotten what he'd told her the day before—the vile tale he'd woven of her beloved friend. In the aftermath, she was unsettled, unsure, but she wanted to make it clear that she hadn't accepted his story.

She wasn't sure she ever could.

Gradually, the pile of shells beside the glowing fire grew, and eventually, they finished the last handful of shellfish.

Astrid's belly was full now, a relief indeed.

Sitting back, she wiped her mouth and chin with the back of her hand. It occurred to her then that, as delicious as their meal had been, there wouldn't be an endless supply of shellfish. However, sourcing food wasn't the biggest problem for them. There was little fuel for fire upon this barren isle, and their only fresh water supply was the trickle that ran down the cave wall.

"What is it?"

Astrid looked up to find Finn observing her. His expression was shuttered, yet, as often, his eyes were sharp, assessing.

"Just contemplating our future upon this isle." She swallowed, as fear tightened her throat. "It wasn't a happy thought."

Finn's lean face tensed. "Aye … there's a reason why no one has ever bothered to settle here."

Astrid's full belly churned. "I can't imagine never seeing Duart again … or Loch and Mairi." Her voice caught then. "Maybe Loch will send out a search party."

"Aye," Finn replied, his gaze holding hers. "He might … if he survives the coming days."

Astrid's stomach pitched once more. "I only just got him back," she said, severing eye contact then. "It's not fair."

"Not much in life is."

Astrid cut Finn a sharp look. "Ye aren't helping, MacDonald. Is there anything that comes out of yer mouth that isn't cynical?"

He snorted yet didn't dignify her with a response.

Astrid's gaze narrowed, her fear and dread drawing back as she focused on the vexing man seated opposite. "How does a man get such a dark view of the world?"

His eyes glinted. "Oh, I don't know … being accused of a crime ye didn't commit might do it."

Astrid stiffened. She wasn't going to discuss Maggie with him again. "Maybe … but that isn't the only reason ye sneer at the world. Ye were always distrustful … even when ye first arrived at Duart."

He shrugged. "It's my nature."

"What? To be unpleasant?"

His gaze narrowed, his mouth thinning. "Perhaps ... why do ye think my parents sent me away?"

Despite her simmering temper, Finn's response intrigued Astrid. "They sent ye to foster at Duart to *rid* themselves of ye?"

"Aye."

Astrid harrumphed. "Surely not ... ye were only seven when ye turned up at our door."

"Old enough to be a terror. I'm the youngest of five sons ... the difficult one my parents never knew what to do with. My father tried to beat it out of me, but that just made me sneaky ... so when the chance to have one of his sons foster at Duart arose, he eagerly took it."

His words surprised Astrid. How had she not known this about him? Silence fell between them for a few moments before she cleared her throat. "So, ye believe ye were *born* with a poor character?"

Finn made an irritated sound in the back of his throat. "We can stop talking about me now."

Astrid drew herself up. "Not when the conversation is this interesting. Answer my question, MacDonald, and ye can ask me a thorny one too."

His eyebrows shot up. "Is this a game now?"

Astrid pulled a face. "Hardly ... but since we're stuck together, we might as well entertain ourselves. Otherwise, there will be a lot of silence in the coming days."

"I like silence."

"Just humor me."

14: JUST ONE QUESTION

FINN LEANED BACK on his hands and stretched his long legs out in front of him, crossing them at the ankle. "Aye, I was likely born this way," he answered grudgingly. "From as early as I can remember, my mother told me so."

"What did she say?"

Finn frowned, clearly bristling at her questioning. "That's *two* questions, Astrid."

"Aye, but it's linked to the first, so we'll allow it."

Finn muttered an oath under his breath, yet Astrid pretended not to hear. Despite everything, she was genuinely curious about this man's origins. She wasn't sure why—perhaps the isolation was getting to her.

"She said I was demanding from the first," he replied, his tone gruff now. "That unlike my brothers, I cried all the time." His hazel eyes narrowed then. "Her answer was to leave me bawling, for hours at a time, I'm told. Then, when I grew from a wee bairn to a lad, I was prone to fits of temper ... so my nurse locked me in a store cupboard until I calmed down. None of it helped though. I grew up wild, argumentative, and sly. My father smiled the day he put me on the boat to Mull."

Astrid's breathing grew shallow at this tale. Finn talked as if his upbringing didn't bother him at all, yet to her, his childhood sounded horrific. Loch, too, had been a difficult child, but their parents hadn't resorted to such treatment.

"Yer kin sound vile," she admitted after a pause, momentarily forgetting to be wary around him. "I can't imagine ye missed them."

He gave a humorless laugh. "I didn't ... I still don't."

They ceased talking then, the crackle and pop of the fire between them mingling with the rumble of the surf. The tide had turned now, and waves rolled in close to shore.

Eventually, Astrid cleared her throat. "Well, ye have the chance to ask me anything ye like," she said, suddenly wishing she hadn't made such an offer. She didn't trust the gleam in Finn's eyes. "Go on."

"I'm thinking," he replied.

Astrid pursed her lips. "Really?"

"Aye." He continued to observe her then before inclining his head. "Have ye ever pined for anyone, Astrid?"

Her spine snapped rigid. "What kind of question is that?" she muttered, even as panic forked like lightning through her.

Finn cocked an eyebrow. "Ye said I could ask ye *anything*."

Astrid wanted to snarl at him, to tell him that whether she'd pined for anyone was her business and no one else's. Indeed, the knave could have asked her anything— just not this.

Silence fell once more between them until Finn finally made an impatient noise in the back of his throat. "Come on ... a man could grow old and die waiting for yer answer."

"Aye ... I did want someone once," she admitted, deliberately looking away from him. "Years ago though ... when I was young."

"Ye are still young, Astrid."

"Aye, but this was when I was fifteen."

"And who was he?"

Her jaw clenched. "Just one question, remember?"

"Aye, but ye slipped in a second one, and so shall I."

Astrid ground her teeth, even as the urge to scramble to her feet, pick up her skirts, and flee spiked through her.

Christ's blood, she couldn't believe she was conversing with Finn at all, let alone that their exchange had taken them here, to the very subject she'd spent a lifetime burying. These days, she didn't even admit to herself that she'd ever suffered that infatuation.

"No one of importance," she said, her tone clipped now as she struggled to rein in her panic.

Finn harrumphed. "That's no answer."

A sickly sensation washed over Astrid then, and her hands turned clammy. Steeling herself, she looked back at Finn, her belly clenching when she found his gaze locked on her. The bastard wasn't going to let this go—one way or another, he intended to get the truth out of her. She didn't understand his curiosity. What did he care about her silly girlhood infatuations?

And so, drawing in a deep breath, she gave him her answer. "All right then, MacDonald ... here's yer answer. It was *ye*."

Finn's reaction was almost comical. His mouth dropped open, his eyebrows shooting up to his hairline.

For a moment, Astrid almost laughed, and then she remembered just how mortifying it was to admit such a thing to the man she now considered her enemy.

The day before, when he'd told her that it was her, rather than Maggie, he'd been interested in, it had stirred old memories.

Aye, she'd been jealous that day on the road back from Craignure, when Maggie had flirted with Finn—but not just because she was potentially losing her friend's attention. Maggie had found it so easy to talk to lads she liked, while Astrid was hopeless. Virile young men with hungry eyes had made her nervous and tongue-tied. What an irony that she prided herself on her negotiation skills these days yet had once struggled to meet a lad's eye.

"It's hard to believe, isn't it?" she said softly.

Finn shut his mouth before nodding. However, his eyes were still wide, startled. He was looking at her now as if she'd just taken off a mask to reveal a completely different identity.

"Maggie was always the chatty one." She dropped her gaze to her lap, developing a sudden fascination with her fingers, which she was currently twisting into knots. "She loved flirting, but I didn't. I was painfully shy back then ... so, I decided it was better to act aloof, to pretend I wasn't interested in anyone. The more I liked a lad, the colder I behaved."

Finn murmured another curse, and Astrid glanced up. His eyes had narrowed slightly. "I thought ye barely noticed I breathed," he murmured.

Astrid huffed a bitter laugh. "Oh, I *noticed* ye, Finn ... and it tore me up when ye started spending time with Maggie." Her mouth twisted then. "However, after she drowned, my tenderness toward ye twisted into hate. It was a silly, childish infatuation anyway, and would have passed with time."

She looked away from Finn then, as the intense way he was watching her made her feel nervous. Enough of these probing, difficult questions. It was her fault for starting it, but it was time to stop this conversation.

Both of them had already said too much.

However, when Astrid's gaze alighted upon the horizon, she froze.

A moment later, her heart kicked hard against her breastbone. "Finn!" she gasped, struggling to her feet. "Look!"

He twisted around, rising to stand next to her—and when he caught sight of the speck on the horizon, his breathing caught. "A ship."

15: FLYING THE BLOODY FLAG

"AYE." EXCITEMENT BUBBLED up inside Astrid before desperation joined it. "But they're too far away ... they'll never see us."

"We need to feed the fire ... and get some smoke billowing," Finn replied, his voice sharpening. Their revealing conversation was now forgotten, especially since their only hope of escaping this rock was on the horizon. "Start feeding the rest of our wood to the fire while I gather some more. Hurry!"

He didn't need to tell Astrid twice. With a nod, she rushed to the pile of driftwood Finn had carried down from the cave and started to add pieces to the glowing embers, poking the fire to rouse it.

Meanwhile, Finn took off, still barefoot, down the sand in search of more fuel.

Astrid worked feverishly, coaxing the flames high, as she constantly glanced out to sea. The ship was still visible, traveling along the horizon. But how long would it be before it slipped over the edge of the world?

Finn returned a short time later, with more driftwood and a large piece of dried kelp. "We need the fire to smoke ... or they'll never see us," he said, adding the items he'd brought to the burning pyre. "Some damp seaweed should do it."

"Right." Leaving Finn to tend the fire, Astrid shot away, running in the opposite direction to what he had earlier, to where a tangle of wet kelp lay on the sand. It was heavy, so she grabbed one end and dragged it behind her, back to the fire.

"Well done," Finn greeted her. He then withdrew his dirk from its sheath at his hip and cut the length of kelp up before feeding it, piece by piece, onto the roaring fire.

Moments later, it began to smoke, sending billowing dark clouds high into the noon sky.

Standing on the waterline, peering at the horizon, Astrid gave a whoop. "The ship is turning ... they've seen us!"

"Thank Christ!"

Sure enough, the speck on the horizon was getting larger. With each moment, its shape grew more defined. Initially, Astrid had thought it was a birlinn, yet as it drew closer, its single sail billowing in the wind, she noted its high clinkered sides. "It looks like a merchant's cog," she called out to Finn before swallowing a sob of relief. She couldn't believe it.

Fate wasn't set against them, after all.

She gave a squeal of joy and leaped in the air, clapping her hands.

Finn stepped up next to her then, abandoning the fire now that they'd attracted attention. Astrid spun toward him, meeting his eye, and for a moment, they grinned at each other, momentarily bonded by relief.

Then, to her surprise, he placed his hands on her waist, picked her up, and spun her around—and she laughed, jubilation flooding through her.

They were saved. Once the cog picked them up, she'd do all she could to ensure they got passage to Skye. Loch would get the help he needed.

They were both grinning as Finn put her down. However, their smiles faded when their gazes met.

Warmth ignited in Astrid's belly as their stare drew out, and then she became aware of just how close he was standing. It was disconcerting, and her breathing grew shallow. Lord, the way he was looking at her now was far too intimate—and yet, suddenly, she couldn't break their gaze.

And then, Finn caught her by the waist once more and drew her close. The next instant, his mouth was on hers.

Astrid gasped at the feel of his lips, surprisingly soft yet firm, against her own. But her shock expanded when his tongue slid between them and sought entrance into her mouth.

The act was intimate and bold. She should have jerked away, should have slapped his brazen face, but instead, her lips parted, and she allowed his tongue in. It delved, stroked, and explored.

Before Astrid knew what she was doing, she was kissing him back.

Hungrily. Feverishly.

His mouth tasted of the sea and of him. Astrid welcomed his questing tongue and the feel of the rough stubble that covered his jaw rasping against her sensitive skin. Her hands came up, splaying across his chest. Through the thin material of his lèine, she felt the heat of his body and the thunder of his heart.

Mother Mary, what was this? His embrace made her giddy, set a fire alight in her lower belly, and made her toes curl into the sand. Astrid had never been kissed. Aye, she'd wondered many times what it would be like to have a man's mouth on hers yet would never have guessed that Finn would be her first.

That thought roused her from the enchantment, reminding her of where they were—of *who* they were.

Pushing back on Finn's chest, Astrid stepped away from him. He let her go, dropping his hands from her waist.

For a few moments, they merely stared at each other, breathing hard.

Astrid saw her own shock mirrored in his gaze. His act had been instinctive, it seemed, and in the aftermath, he had no words. Even so, it was hard not to stare at his mouth, not to step into the cage of his arms again and welcome his embrace once more.

But they'd both forgotten themselves, and it was time to return to reality.

God's blood, this was the man she held responsible for Maggie's death. What was she doing kissing him?

Face flushing, as mortification flooded over her in a hot tide, Astrid looked back at where the cog approached.

She could see it clearly now. The large woven wool sail was emerald-green, and she could make out the outlines of men at the railings. "There's a red flag atop its mast," she noted aloud, cursing her husky voice, and fighting to forget the torrid kiss she'd just shared with the man she hated.

Astrid's breathing caught, and suddenly, it was as if someone had just upended a pail of icy seawater over her head.

All her elation drained out of her, as did her embarrassment.

Finn ground out a curse then, making it clear he'd seen it too. "Satan's cods … they're flying the 'Bloody Flag'."

Astrid's heart started to pound wildly.

They both looked on as the cog sailed closer still and then dropped anchor. They could see the crew clearly now; most of them were clad roughly, their long, unkempt hair tangling in the wind. And as they lowered a rowboat full of men, Astrid's pulse took off like a bolting hind.

"God help us," she whispered. "What are we going to do?"

Both she and Finn started backing up then, moving away from where the water lapped the sand.

"There's no point in running," Finn pointed out roughly. "This isle is too small to hide from them."

"So, we just wait here and let the pirates attack us?"

Sweat bathed Astrid's skin now. She'd recently met the mercenary Logan Black, who'd sailed a cog that looked a lot like this one. Some folk had called the man a pirate, but he wasn't really—more a privateer with a bone to pick against the Mackinnons. But Black no longer sailed the seas. He was now the chieftain of Croggan and would have traveled to Dounarwyse to aid her brother.

These men weren't like Black, who'd long been a friend to the Macleans, though. The hungry looks on their faces, gleam in their eyes, and savage grins made fear curl in her gut. They reminded her of the group of men who'd surrounded her on the beach that morning after she fled Duart, months earlier. She'd been looking for passage off Mull so she could escape her impending marriage yet had found trouble instead. The mercenaries had encircled her, their faces twisted with lust and cruelty.

She'd pulled out a blade and cut one of them, holding them at bay for mere moments. However, she'd been outnumbered, and things would have gone ill, indeed, if Loch, Jack, and Finn hadn't rescued her.

Astrid cut Finn a sidelong look then, her heart hammering in her ears. He'd drawn his dirk, and his expression was hard and cold. "Get behind me, Astrid," he muttered, not looking her way.

She swallowed. "There has to be at least eight of them," she pointed out huskily. "Ye'll never best them all."

"They're watching ye like wolves," he replied, a muscle bunching in his lean jaw. "But if they want to claim their prize, they'll have to kill me first."

Panic slammed into Astrid. She then reached down and drew her own dirk. "Ye aren't facing them alone," she muttered, even as her heart lurched into her throat and sweat dampened her armpits and palms.

"Astrid." His voice was a warning growl. "Get back."

"No." Ignoring her roaring pulse, she dropped into a fighting stance. Aye, she was terrified, but she'd fight all the same. She flexed her fingers on the worn bone hilt of her dirk. She'd not stand by and watch them kill him before they threw her down on the sand and raped her.

The sweat that bathed her skin turned cold, and her legs started to shake.

Hold fast! She couldn't let her courage desert her. Not now.

A braver woman would turn the knife upon herself before letting any of these brutes touch her, yet she wasn't strong enough for that.

The rowboat reached the water's edge then, and eight big men disembarked.

Finn muttered another curse. "Keep silent," he warned her. "Let me do the talking."

Despite her churning fear, Astrid bristled at his command. Who did he think he was?

A tall man with wild dark-blond hair and a close-cropped beard led the group of pirates. Clad in a loose lèine tucked into braies and high boots that molded muscular calves, he swaggered toward them with supreme confidence.

His gaze slid over Finn and rested upon Astrid—and the half-smile that curved his mouth stretched into a grin. "What a fierce welcome." His deep voice boomed across the beach, above the roar of the surf behind him. "Anyone would think ye two were protecting buried treasure."

"There's no treasure on this rock," Finn replied, drawing the pirate's attention once more. Cutting her companion another glance, Astrid noted how Finn's fingers flexed around the hilt of his dirk. "Just two shipwreck survivors."

The pirate's gait slowed, his dark-blond eyebrows rising. Behind him, his crewmates exchanged looks. "Aye?"

"Our birlinn came to grief in that vicious storm two days ago," Astrid added.

She felt Finn's sharp look in her direction yet ignored him. This was *her* mission, and she'd be the one to talk their way out of this mess.

"Aye, and what a tempest it was." The pirate halted, his long hair tangling in the wind. His gaze then raked over her, from head to foot, taking in every detail. Astrid stared back, even as something inside her quailed. His predatory look made her feel as if she were standing naked before him. "Who are ye, lass?"

"Lady Astrid of the Macleans of Duart," she replied, drawing herself up and squaring her shoulders, even as her legs were now shaking worse than ever. "And sister to the clan-chief." She paused then, swallowing hard. "And ye?"

The pirate gazed back at her for a heartbeat longer before he flashed her another wolfish grin. "Ye have the pleasure of meeting Alec Rankin," he drawled. "Legendary spùinneadair-mara and bane of the Western Isles himself."

16: A PIRATE'S HONOR

THE ARROGANCE OF the man's introduction made Finn's lips thin.

Spùinneadair-mara indeed. Like most folk, he'd heard of this infamous 'plunderer of the seas'.

Alec Rankin had carved quite a name for himself in the Western Isles over the past decade, and indeed, the cur knew the mere sight of his ship, *The Blood Reiver*, struck fear into most men's hearts.

Finn wasn't immune to this man's fearsome reputation either.

His pulse now hammered in his ears, although his fear wasn't for himself. Loch had charged him with Astrid's protection, yet he was about to fail them both. It didn't help that his charge refused to take orders from him—Astrid was infuriating enough to make him want to wring her neck.

Instead, he'd kissed her. Christ's bones, what had possessed him? One moment, he'd been grinning at her, relieved that they wouldn't be marooned forever upon this godforsaken rock, the next, the urge to kiss her had swept over him—an urge so strong that he'd given in to it.

Rankin's attention shifted from Astrid to Finn then, his sea-green eyes narrowing. "And ye are?"

"Finn MacDonald. Captain of the Duart Guard."

"We lost the rest of our crew during the storm," Astrid cut in. "Ye haven't picked up anyone else, have ye?"

The pirate glanced her way once more before shaking his head.

Astrid's eyes guttered at this, while grief twinged deep in Finn's chest. *Curse that vile tempest.*

"We're on our way to Dunvegan Castle on Skye," Astrid continued, her voice husky with sorrow. "It's a matter of urgency."

The pirate captain inclined his head then, his gaze narrowing. "And why the hurry?"

"The Mackinnons of Dùn Ara have attacked the Macleans of Dounarwyse ... and my brother sent me to get help from our allies on Skye."

Alec Rankin's lips lifted at the edges. "So, ye think the Macleods of Dunvegan will rush to yer aid?"

"Aye, that is our hope." The pirate captain's gaze glinted at these words, but Astrid pressed on. "Time is short, we must get to Skye ... will ye take us?"

Rankin folded his arms across his broad chest. He then glanced over his shoulder at his men. "What do ye think, lads ... shall we give these two passage to Skye?" The man behind him waggled his eyebrows, while another leered. Someone else then muttered something coarse.

Finn's gut hardened, his fingers flexing on the hilt of his dirk once more. He'd cut up their smirking faces if they continued to disrespect Astrid.

However, if their response unsettled his companion, she didn't show it.

Instead, she let them snigger, waiting until their captain focused on her once more before she lifted her chin and eyeballed him. "Are ye a man of honor, Rankin?"

He snorted. "I'm a *pirate*, lass."

"Aye, but I've heard it said that even a spùinneadair-mara has a moral code."

His self-assured smile slipped at that, while Finn silently congratulated Astrid on her response. Indeed, the pirates that sailed the Western Isles were a proud lot; many of them were men banished from their clans who had nothing to lose. Yet Highland blood flowed through their veins—and to a Highlander, honor was all.

Astrid had hit a raw nerve.

"The Macleans are in desperate need," Astrid said then, taking a bold step forward. "And I call upon ye to help us."

Silence settled then, swelling like the incoming tide.

Finn tensed. He admired Astrid's spine, yet he worried she might have gone too far. She didn't know Alec Rankin. Maybe he had a reason to dislike the Macleans.

"How many silver pennies does the purse at yer waist contain?" the pirate asked eventually.

Finn clenched his jaw at Rankin's mercenary question.

However, Astrid didn't bat an eyelid. "Fifty-five."

Finn's already fast pulse quickened further. Curse it, that coin was to be used to sweeten the Macleods, just in case Tormod wasn't inclined to be generous with his assistance. After all, he hadn't made Loch any promises.

Rankin's mouth tugged into an arrogant grin. "Well then … it looks like ye've just bought yerself some honor."

Astrid couldn't believe it.

Alec Rankin had agreed to take them to Skye. Aye, it took some silver in the end, but she'd still managed to convince him.

Astrid was quietly proud of what she'd achieved. Nonetheless, her heart had been in her throat as she and Finn followed him and his crew to the rowboat, her nervousness intensifying further when she set foot on *The Blood Reiver's* deck.

What if Rankin was playing with them?

What if he turned nasty the moment they stepped aboard his cog?

However, he and his warriors had merely clambered out of the rowboat after them, and the captain busied himself shouting orders to his men. They lifted the boat onto the deck and strapped it down before raising anchor and setting sail north.

Standing upon the forecastle—the raised deck at the bow— her cloak wrapped tightly around her, Astrid watched the lonely isle disappear behind them.

Finn stepped up next to her, and their gazes met.

"Do ye think we're safe onboard this ship?" she whispered. Around them, the crew of *The Blood Reiver* were all too busy to pay them much attention. Rankin had climbed up to the castle at the stern of the ship, where he now stood at the great wooden wheel that steered the cog.

"No," Finn replied, stepping closer—near enough that she could feel the heat of his body burning into her. Astrid's breathing caught. The memory of their kiss was still fresh, and his nearness knocked her off balance. Kissing him was a mistake though; they'd both been giddy with relief and joy and neither of them was thinking clearly. "Never trust a pirate."

Her pulse spiked. "Ye think I should have negotiated harder with him?"

Finn stared down at her before he favored her with a tight smile. "No, ye did the right thing ... I just chafe at the idea of handing coin over to the bastard."

"I had little choice, ye realize?" she replied dryly. "Let's face it, he could have taken it from me by force."

"I'd have cut off his hand if he'd laid a finger on ye."

Astrid's breathing hitched at this declaration. "Fortunately, there was no need for that."

"No." Finn gave his head a rueful shake then. "That was a clever trick though ... appealing to his sense of honor. Ye handled him well."

Their gazes held, and Astrid's pulse quickened further. Curse it. Finn's scorn was much easier to deal with than his compliments. Confusion swept over her then. She didn't understand what was happening between them, and she much preferred it when they were snarling at each other—that, at least, she knew how to deal with.

Yet the shipwreck had altered their relationship. In the past two days, they'd admitted secrets to each other, had learned things about their enemy that made it difficult to ever see them in the same light again.

Astrid didn't want to believe his tale about Maggie—and indeed, she fought against it with every part of her being—but now she was starting to suspect he hadn't lied to her.

She didn't want to consider what that meant. Guilt stabbed at her whenever she thought about Maggie—and about what she'd done to Finn in the aftermath of her friend's death.

But that wasn't all of it. Finn had once pined for her. He'd also learned that *she'd* been infatuated with *him* years earlier—and in the excitement of seeing their rescuers approach, they'd kissed.

Life had been easier when he'd been her nemesis.

She'd enjoyed hating him. Anger made her feel strong and righteous—in control. She wanted to dredge up the old loathing once more, but the earnestness in his hazel eyes made her falter, and so she merely favored him with a nod of thanks and cut her gaze away.

"We should reach Dunvegan at dusk," Alec Rankin announced, taking a gulp from his cup of ale, "although ye'll forgive me for not dropping ye off at the sea gate."

"And why is that?" Finn asked.

They sat at a sturdy oaken table—sharing a simple meal of bread, cheese, and ale with Rankin—in a large paneled room located under the castle, at the bow of the cog. A heavy curtain hid the back of the space, presumably where the captain slept.

Finn had been on edge ever since stepping onto *The Blood Reiver*, and breaking bread with its captain didn't ease the knots in his gut.

"I'm not popular with the Macleods of Skye," Rankin replied with a devil-may-care shrug. "So, it's best I leave ye at a cove south of Dunvegan ... ye can walk the rest of the way."

Finn gave a slow nod, even as suspicion grew like gathering storm clouds inside him.

Honor be damned, he didn't trust this man.

"Why are ye helping us, Rankin?" he demanded, trying to ignore the hunk of bread on the trencher in front of him that was making his mouth water.

Astrid shot him a warning look, but he pretended not to notice. There was something Rankin wasn't telling them.

"For fifty-five silver pennies," the captain replied, spearing a piece of cheese with his eating knife. "And a pirate's honor." He grinned then, amused by his own quip.

"Ye have a fearsome reputation," Astrid spoke up. Her brow was furrowed as her gaze met Rankin's. "They say ye rape and pillage yer way across the Western Isles."

Rankin's grin faded. "Ye shouldn't believe everything ye hear. We plunder, aye ... but we don't rape." He paused then, a groove etching between his brows. "My crew all know that their lives are forfeit if they ravish anyone."

"So, ye have *morals*?" Finn couldn't help the derision that crept into his voice. Next, the pirate would tell them he gave the wealth he stole to abbeys.

Rankin glanced his way, his gaze narrowing. "Not many of them ... but when I was a lad, my elder sister was raped by a local lout ... and I killed him for it." The quiet menace in his voice shivered across the chamber. "I'm no saint, MacDonald, but there are some lines I won't cross." He shrugged then. "Besides, it suits me for folk to believe I'm a beast ... they hand over their coin faster that way."

The pirate let his words lie and returned to his supper.

Meanwhile, Finn ripped off a piece of bread and took a bite. Next to him, Astrid ate hungrily.

They were halfway through their meal when Rankin leaned back against the paneled wall, surveying his guests. "There *is* another reason I agreed to give ye passage," he admitted softly.

Finn raised his cup to his lips and took a gulp of bitter ale, even as his pulse quickened. *Here we go.* "Aye?"

"I met Iain Maclean once." Rankin's mouth quirked into a half-smile as he glanced Astrid's way. "When I was a lad, looking for trouble on the docks at Oban, I tried to lift his coin purse, but he caught me." Rankin paused there, grimacing at the memory. "I thought he'd give me a beating, but he didn't. Instead, he hunkered down so our eyes were level and cast his gaze over me—no doubt taking in my grimy skin, threadbare clothes, and puniness—before he asked where my Da was. I told him the truth … that he'd drunk himself to death after my Ma died. There was only my sister and me left."

Rankin halted here and took a pull of ale before flashing Astrid a rueful smile. "Yer Da surprised me once again by taking a silver penny from his purse and pressing it into my palm. He then told me that if in the future I was going to steal a man's coin, I should look him in the eye when I did it."

Astrid raised an eyebrow. "And so ye took his advice?"

Rankin's smile widened. "Aye."

17: A WOMAN OF YER WORD

THEY SAILED UP the west coast of Skye, past rocky coves, plunging cliffs, and emerald-green headlands with sculped peaks thrusting into the sky behind them.

And despite that she was anxious to reach her destination, Skye's fabled beauty enchanted Astrid. She'd visited this isle once—when she'd been little more than a bairn, with Loch and her parents—yet she didn't recall just how breathtaking it was.

Turning her thoughts from worries about what was happening on Mull, she focused instead upon the magnificent razor-sharp, smoky peaks to the east then, which sliced into a limpid sky. Sunlight highlighted the steep sides and deep corries. Ironically, the weather had been glorious ever since the tempest, late spring turning into summer.

"The Black Cuillin are a sight, are they not?"

Tearing her gaze away from the mountains, Astrid glanced right to find that Rankin was standing at her shoulder.

Finn was a few feet away. Ever since the pirate captain had made it clear he owed Astrid's father a favor, he'd relaxed a little. However, glancing left, Astrid marked the way her protector's gaze narrowed.

He was still suspicious of Rankin, it seemed.

Shifting her attention back to the pirate, Astrid favored him with a wary smile. "Aye ... I've never seen mountains of the like ... not even Ben More on Mull can rival them."

"They sit within the Macleod borders," Rankin replied. "Our destination isn't far away."

Astrid inclined her head, studying him now. "What did ye do to make yerself an enemy of Tormod Macleod?"

The pirate flashed her a grin, revealing surprisingly white and even teeth. "What I've done from one end of the Western

Isles to the other," he boasted. "More than one Macleod birlinn has crossed our path over the years ... and when they do, we help ourselves to their bounty." He paused then. "When ye get to Dunvegan ... best ye tell them a merchant picked ye up."

Astrid stiffened, ignoring his advice as she focused on his admission instead. "And what of the crews of the galleys ye attack?"

Rankin's grin faded, his bright blue eyes hardening.

Astrid suppressed a shudder. He didn't need to say a word—she had her answer.

Silence fell between them for a short while before Astrid eventually cut the pirate a sidelong glance. "Ye got a goodly amount of silver out of me, Rankin," she murmured, "But ye were always going to take us weren't ye ... thanks to yer association with my father?"

Their gazes held before he favored her with a half-smile. "Aye, but the coin is much appreciated, all the same."

Astrid's mouth pursed.

Rankin stepped closer then. "May I be frank with ye, Lady Astrid?"

"I suppose so," she replied, eyeing him warily.

"Ye put on a brave face before the world ... yet I sense the uncertainty just beneath. Ye doubt yerself, don't ye?"

Astrid's pulse leaped. Rankin had only known her a short while—how had he managed to cut straight to the core of who she was? She considered deflecting him with a flippant comment yet stopped herself. It wasn't his fault that he'd seen the truth. "Aye," she answered after a moment. "Sometimes."

"Why? Ye are sharp-witted and capable."

She huffed a soft laugh. "Aye ... but it's what lies in the heart that matters. Ye are right ... I'm not half as tough as I appear." She halted, swallowing. "Deep down ... I'm a coward."

Hades, she couldn't believe she'd admitted such a thing to him. To a stranger.

He arched an eyebrow. "Ye have survived a shipwreck, Lady Astrid ... don't be so hard on yerself."

She gave a soft snort. "Captain MacDonald is largely responsible for that ... and fate took care of the rest."

"Ye brood too much," Rankin replied with a shrug. "Getting tangled in yer thoughts never does anyone good."

Astrid frowned. The pirate was free with his opinions.

Nonetheless, he wasn't yet finished. "Trust yer gut a little more, lass. When ye need it, courage will find ye."

The Blood Reiver dropped anchor at a small cove where pines and birch grew down to the water.

The pirates, their captain among them, rowed Astrid and Finn out to the pebbly beach where they alighted.

Rankin stepped off the boat too, awaiting his payment.

Astrid untied the purse from her belt and handed it to him. "It's all there," she assured him. "Although ye are welcome to count it, if ye wish."

The pirate flashed her a grin. "No need for that. I can see ye are a woman of yer word." He stepped toward her then, his fingers closing around the purse. "However, if ye wish to pay me with a kiss as well, I won't decline."

Astrid stilled, her eyes widening at his boldness.

Meanwhile, next to her, Finn's reaction surprised her even more than the pirate's behavior.

He actually *growled*. "Touch her, Rankin ... and I shall cut off yer balls."

Astrid stifled a gasp and shifted her attention to Finn, to find him glaring at the pirate, a murderous look on his lean face, his eyes narrowed into slits.

Hades, he looked a breath away from making good on his threat.

Rankin, on the other hand, merely chuckled and stepped back. "Ye need to keep yer hound on a tighter leash, Lady Astrid," he said mildly. "Or he's likely to bite someone."

Astrid drew in a deep breath. "Very well, Rankin," she said finally. "Ye'll get a kiss from me ... and a bag of *one hundred* silver pennies as well ... if ye agree to sail south after ye leave us and go to my brother's aid."

Next to her, another growl rumbled deep in Finn's throat, but Astrid didn't look his way. Instead, her gaze remained fixed upon the pirate.

Let Finn growl. The Macleans were desperate for help—and she didn't care from whence it came. After all, the Macleods couldn't be counted on.

Rankin held her gaze, surprise flickering across his face. "A generous offer indeed, Lady Astrid," he murmured after a lengthy pause. "But one I must decline. I don't like to involve myself in the conflicts between clans."

"Why not?" she demanded, not ready to let this go. Rankin had a large ship and a hardy crew. He also wasn't as villainous as the legends surrounding him told. Loch wouldn't turn their assistance away.

As if reading her thoughts, Rankin's mouth curved. "That's the way I like it, lass … and the way it will remain."

"Careful, Astrid," Finn muttered once the pirates had climbed back into their boat and were rowing back to *The Blood Reiver*. "Ye were playing a dangerous game there."

Snorting, Astrid turned to her companion. "I wasn't. I was offering Rankin a job."

"And offering yerself as part payment." Anger glinted in his eyes.

Astrid folded her arms across her chest. "It was just a kiss."

"A man like Rankin will take more than that," he countered.

She made an exasperated sound in the back of her throat. "For the love of God, MacDonald … I can do without ye snarling at my shoulder while I try to negotiate."

"The bastard overstepped."

Astrid's mouth pursed, her temper quickening. "Maybe, but I was handling him in my own way."

Finn screwed his face up and stepped away from her, motioning to the path that led up a steep bank into the trees. "Come on," he snapped. "We can argue while we walk."

Astrid picked up her skirts and brushed past him, bristling now. "I'm not arguing with ye."

"Always have to get the last word, don't ye?" he answered, following her.

Astrid flung a venomous look over her shoulder. "And *ye* don't?"

Quietly fuming, she strode up the hill. It was best she didn't engage with Finn at all. Now that they were out of immediate danger, there was no need for them to converse, for when they did, things always seemed to go into a spiral.

And his reaction when Alec Rankin had requested a kiss had been feral—almost as if he was jealous.

Astrid's pulse lurched into a canter. *Jealous?*

Aye, they'd kissed, but that didn't give MacDonald any claim over her.

They walked on, following the coastline north before the pines drew back and a castle appeared ahead. Built upon a rocky outcrop, a dove-grey keep with a high curtain wall stood against a cloudy sky. The fortress overlooked an inlet with a long wooden jetty, where several birlinns were moored.

Astrid surveyed their destination as she made her way along the path toward the steep, rocky steps that led up to the castle's sea gate. Although Dunvegan lacked Duart Castle's lofty position, Astrid had to admit that this stronghold also had a commanding presence.

The Macleods of Dunvegan were renowned, and feared, throughout the Highlands, and for good reason too.

Astrid's belly clenched as her gaze flicked to the galleys bobbing with the tide. She had to get Tormod Macleod's assistance, and quickly.

Drawing in a deep breath, she glanced right at where Finn walked next to her. His attention was riveted on their destination, a groove etched between his eyebrows.

"When we go before the clan-chief, *I* will do all the talking," Astrid informed him then.

Finn's gaze snapped to her, his jaw bunching. "What's wrong ... ye don't trust me?"

She didn't actually, not after his outburst earlier. "This mission is vital," she replied, her chin lifting. "Tormod might be reluctant to aid us ... and Loch's counting on me to get the help we need."

"I know just how important this is," Finn countered, his eyebrows drawing together. "And I may not be a Maclean, but I care about what happens to yer clan as much as ye do."

Astrid's eyes widened. "Ye do? I thought yer loyalty was to my brother ... and Jack ... and no one else."

His mouth thinned. "Maybe ... once," he replied, cutting his attention away, back to the castle that now reared above them. From here, they could see helmed figures on the walls, staring down at them.

"But not any longer?" Astrid kicked herself for continuing to engage him in conversation. Nonetheless, she couldn't help herself. Curse him, Finn intrigued her. He was a man of many layers. Once she stripped back one, there was another, even more intriguing, underneath.

Intriguing? Hades, where was her mind leading her these days?

Finn shook his head, still not looking her way. "I will serve yer clan for as long as Loch will put up with me," he answered gruffly. Then, before she could ask him anything further, Finn strode ahead, climbing the rocky path up to the sea gate.

"The Saints were looking after ye, lass," Tormod Macleod announced, his rheumy grey eyes sweeping down Astrid's no doubt bedraggled form. Her surcote and cloak were both stained and stiff with salt. Underneath her clothing, her skin itched. "That was a devil of a storm."

"Aye, it passed this way first," the clan-chief's son, Malcolm, added. "And smashed two of our birlinns to pieces on the rocks before it moved south."

Astrid's stomach swooped at this news. They needed as much help as the Macleods of Dunvegan were prepared to give. However, if they'd lost two of their galleys, Tormod might be hesitant to assist them.

"We were fortunate indeed," she agreed, her gaze resting once more on the clan-chief's face. She'd heard Tormod was elderly but wasn't prepared for just how decrepit the man was. Hunched and frail, he looked as if a puff of wind could blow him over. His beard was snow-white and so long that he'd tucked it into his belt. And when he'd entered the great hall to receive them, he leaned heavily on a carven stick.

Nonetheless, the moment Tormod Macleod spoke, the strength of his voice told Astrid that the man still had his wits about him. Disconcertingly, he hadn't smiled once since meeting with her. They now sat together at the clan-chief's table, at one end of a rectangular space with dark paneled walls, a large hearth where a log smoldered, and massive beams that rose above them like a ribcage.

In contrast to his decrepit father, his nineteen-year-old son was hale and strong.

There was no denying that Malcolm Macleod was attractive. Broad-shouldered and powerfully built with a mane of thick auburn hair and piercing grey eyes, he exuded a warrior's arrogance.

When he'd stridden into the hall at his father's heels, Astrid had marked the way the young man's gaze snapped to her, and the interest that had sparked in those slate-grey eyes an instant later.

"Ye are here to ask for our help, Lady Astrid," Tormod said then, his gaze roaming her face. His expression grew stern then. "Aren't ye?"

Astrid nodded. Tormod wasn't one to bandy words, it seemed. However, his manner was worryingly cool. Of course, what she had to say wouldn't entirely be a surprise to him. Loch had corresponded frequently with the Macleod clan-chief over the last few months; she knew her brother had mentioned the brewing trouble with their neighbors.

"The Mackinnons of Dùn Ara have attacked Dounarwyse broch, just a short distance north from Duart," she informed him. "After their clan-chief lost the support of the MacDonalds of Sleat, he delayed his attack ... but he's found new allies now ... and a fleet of birlinns has converged upon us."

Both Tormod and his son's gazes widened at this.

"Whom has he rallied?" the clan-chief asked.

"The MacNabs and the MacGregors," Finn replied. "And it looks as if they've given the Mackinnons everything they have."

Silence followed this announcement, while Astrid resisted the urge to cut Finn a censorious look over her shoulder. She'd told him to let *her* talk to Tormod.

Meanwhile, the clan-chief's gaze remained cool, and a veiled expression dropped over Malcolm's face.

Undaunted, Astrid drew in a deep breath. "My brother is a proud man," she began, her voice low and sure. Aye, she was desperate, for her clan's plight had weighed increasingly upon her ever since *The Blood Reiver* had picked them up. But it was vital not to show any hesitation in meetings like these. "He would never have sent me unless our need was dire." Astrid paused then, allowing her words to settle. However, Tormod's expression didn't change, and neither did his son's.

Astrid's pulse quickened. Hades, this was going to be an even bigger challenge than she'd readied herself for.

Exhaling slowly, she decided it was time to speak plainly. If the old man wasn't one to dress his words up, then neither would she. Instead, she'd remind him of the bond between their clans. "I call upon the old alliance that was forged between ye and my father ... and remind ye that the Macleans of Duart will always stand with ye when ye need us."

Tormod's eyes, cloudy with cataracts, narrowed, but Astrid met the clan-chief's gaze squarely. "Will ye help us?"

18: A CLAN-CHIEF'S PROMISE

"YE ARE ASKING much of us, lass," the clan-chief finally replied, his deep voice rumbling through the hall. The four of them were alone in here, save for an old wolfhound that was currently scratching by the fire. "For it sounds as if the Mackinnons have the upper hand, indeed."

His son nodded at this, clearly agreeing with his father's appraisal of the situation.

Heat washed over Astrid at these words, her temper quickening for the first time since entering Dunvegan Castle. "That's exactly why I'm here," she said, throttling her response. "Why I've braved storms and shipwrecks to reach ye."

"And yer tenacity is impressive," Tormod replied, his expression unchanging. "But I cannot give ye an answer now. First, I must discuss yer request with my son, and my marshal ... alone."

"But my brother needs ye."

"Perhaps." A scowl creased his face now. "Yet Loch will understand that I do not give help blindly. There is much to be considered before I put my birlinns ... and the lives of my men ... at risk."

Swallowing her rising anger, Astrid nodded. It galled her to have to speak softly while Dounarwyse burned. Nonetheless, an aggressive approach would merely vex the clan-chief. She needed to tread carefully now.

The Macleod clan-chief was old, but in his day, he was said to have been one of the most formidable warriors in all of Scotland. Even now, there was a ruthless edge to him, as there was to his son as well.

"I understand yer caution," she said after a pause, "but I must remind ye that my father came to yer aid twenty-two years ago ... and helped ye best the MacDonalds of Sleat."

Tormod's face tightened. "I don't need reminding of that, lass," he snapped. "I might be old, but my wits are intact."

Astrid didn't answer. Her comment had vexed him, yet she couldn't let this exchange conclude without bringing up the past.

Moments slid by, and then Tormod heaved himself up out of his carven chair, using his stick to aid him. "After yer ordeal, ye will both avail yerselves of fine Macleod hospitality," he announced then. "My steward will have chambers prepared for ye and baths drawn." He paused then, his grey eyes sharpening once more as Astrid lifted her chin and met his eye again. "I will give ye my answer at supper this eve."

"Slippery auld bastard ... he's looking for an excuse to refuse us."

Finn's voice, low and hard, vibrated through the bedchamber. The moment the steward, who'd shown them to their lodgings—two chambers connected by a door, had left them, he'd erupted.

Astrid flinched. "Thank the Lord ye didn't say that to his face," she muttered, crossing to a table where a jug of wine and cups had been left. "If Tormod Macleod wants a reason not to help us ... I'd rather ye didn't give him one."

Then, she poured two generous cups of what looked like rich plum wine and carried them across to him. Standing by the open window, Finn took his cup from her. "Thank ye," he said, a little ungraciously.

Facing him, Astrid took a large gulp of wine. Indeed, it was plum—deep and fruity. She needed something to settle her nerves and mounting panic.

What was happening back on Mull? Were they already too late?

"I agree, Tormod's reaction is ... disappointing," she admitted, throttling her fears. "But all isn't lost."

Finn's brow furrowed. "Ye think he'll actually aid us?"

Astrid's breathing grew shallow. "I'm going to do everything in my power to ensure he does."

Their gazes fused then, and Finn's eyes glinted. Was that respect she saw glimmer briefly? Surely not. "Aye, well, choose yer words carefully this eve," he replied, his voice roughening as he took a step closer. "Everything depends on it."

Astrid nodded, a sigh gusting out of her. It had been an exhausting day, full of highs and lows—one moment relief, the next fear and despair. Her mind and body were weary while tension knotted up her insides. "We both need to rest," she replied after a pause. "I must ready myself to lock horns with Tormod."

"And with his son," Finn added. "The cub is as wily as the wolf."

"Aye ... Malcolm says little yet misses nothing. His father will rely on him heavily these days." Astrid's belly twisted then. To calm her nerves, she took another gulp of the delicious plum wine.

Likewise, Finn drank from his cup, although his features remained strained, his gaze still narrowed.

A knock came upon the door then, intruding on their conversation. "Hot water for yer baths," a woman's voice filtered into the chamber.

"Aye," Astrid called out, taking a step back from Finn. Without realizing it, they'd moved inappropriately close to each other.

A moment later, a procession of servants entered, some carrying pails of steaming water, while those at the rear hauled in two large iron tubs—one for her chamber and one for Finn's.

And despite that she was on edge—despite that time was passing and her people still didn't have the help they needed—relief filtered through Astrid.

No, a bath wouldn't solve her problems—yet right now, it was just what she needed.

Sinking down in the large tub, Astrid's eyes fluttered shut. She'd scrubbed her grimy skin clean and washed her hair yet lingered afterward. The water was still deliciously warm, soaking away all her aches and pains. The resinous scent of rosemary, from the oil she'd added to the water, wreathed up, clearing her mind, and strengthening her resolve.

She'd do whatever it took to get help from the Macleods.

Eyes still closed, her head resting on the rolled edge of the iron tub, she went over various arguments in her head, preparing herself for her coming meeting with the clan-chief.

She was deep in thought when the sound of splashing roused her.

Astrid's eyes snapped open, and she glanced right, at the door that separated her and Finn's chambers.

After he'd departed to his room, she deliberately barred the door on her side. However, the only exit from their lodgings was through her chamber, so she'd have to unbar it once she finished bathing.

Her precautions were perhaps a little extreme but Astrid had found it hard to relax, to disrobe and climb naked into the bath, knowing that just an unlocked door lay between them. This chamber and the adjoining one sat on the eastern edge of the keep, designed perhaps for a visiting family.

Aye, Finn was her escort, her protector, but the Macleods didn't need to put him so near her.

Another splash reached her through the door, and Astrid's thoughts strayed.

Suddenly, she was imagining him naked just a few yards away, soaping his skin.

Astrid's pulse quickened.

After they'd washed up upon that deserted isle and stripped off their wet clothes to prevent dying of cold, she'd seen Finn naked. Of course, she'd been too distressed and chilled to be aroused by the sight—and yet, she'd marked it. Finn's body was lean and long. He was narrow-hipped with strong shoulders, finely muscled arms and legs, and a flat abdomen.

She imagined his body now, water trickling down his neck and chest, his skin flushed from heat.

Astrid gave a soft gasp and pushed herself upright with such force that water sloshed over the edge of the tub.

What the devil was she doing?

That kiss they'd shared on the beach had clearly muddled her mind. All the same, her lewd thoughts had caused a strange fluttering low in her belly, followed by a restlessness that made her want to wriggle.

Gritting her teeth, Astrid pulled herself up from the tub and grabbed a drying sheet. She'd ruined her bath. She couldn't continue lazing in the warm water, not if she was going to let her mind travel in such a disturbing direction.

She climbed out of the tub, her feet sinking into a soft sheepskin, and began drying herself off with far more force than was necessary. However, she welcomed the sting of the coarse linen against her skin, for it provided a welcome distraction.

The stress of this mission must be eroding my wits, she consoled herself as she reached for a fresh lèine.

The Macleods put on a fine supper that eve— venison stew, walnut-studded bread, and an array of cheeses—to welcome the Macleans of Mull to Dunvegan. The great hall glowed with warmth, and two musicians—playing a harp and flute high in the minstrels' gallery—performed for the clan-chief, his retainers, and Astrid and Finn.

However, Astrid found it hard to enjoy her meal, the music, or the company. Not when the clan-chief hadn't yet answered her.

Tormod Macleod's warriors and their wives and families lined the long trestle tables beneath the raised dais where the clan-chief's table sat. Making her way through a huge trencher of venison stew—Tormod clearly thought she needed feeding up and had instructed the serving lad to give her a hearty helping—Astrid was aware that gazes kept straying her way.

She pretended not to notice, although she was grateful that she was now clean and wore fresh clothing. It was hard to preserve one's dignity looking like the sea had just spat her out. Of course, the clothing she'd brought with her from Duart Castle was now sitting on the bottom of the sea. Fortunately, their host had provided her with fresh attire.

"That dove-grey surcote is a bonnie one, Lady Astrid," Tormod Macleod spoke up then, drawing her attention. A wistful expression played across his lined face. "My wife, Christina, always looked lovely in it too. She was as slender as ye."

Astrid favored him with a tight smile in return. She didn't want to talk about gowns now, yet she could see that he'd loved his wife. "When did ye lose her?" she asked after a pause. As impatient as she was to speak about more important matters with the clan-chief, she remembered her manners. Despite everything, she was curious about Tormod's life. She had met few folk as old as him. Also, speaking of such things might soften him up.

"Christina was much younger than me, yet a lung sickness claimed her five summers ago now." He paused then. "I look forward to the day we'll be reunited once more."

His comment brought a concerned look from his son, although Tormod ignored it. "I also wish to see my sons Leod and Godfrey again," he admitted, his voice roughening slightly. "Leod died fighting for the Bruce ... and Godfrey was a monk who followed God's call to England, where he died of a fever last winter. Unfortunately, when ye live for as long as I have, too many of those ye love die."

"Ye still have me, Da," Malcolm reminded him, a trifle tersely. The clan-chief's son was seated to Astrid's right this eve, while the clan-chief was to her left. Meanwhile, Finn sat a little farther down the table, with the steward, marshal, and the Captain of the Dunvegan Guard.

"Aye, lad," Tormod rumbled. "And I'm grateful for it."

"Indeed," Astrid said after a pause, breaking off a piece of walnut bread and dipping it in her stew. She favored the clan-chief's son with a smile. "I have heard of yer bravery, Malcolm ... yer skill with a claidheamh-mòr is becoming something of a legend in the Highlands."

Malcolm's handsome face split into a broad grin at these words, while Tormod huffed a wry laugh. "Don't encourage the lad, Lady Astrid ... at just nineteen winters, my son believes he's invincible."

The clan-chief's son raised an eyebrow at this. He then winked at Astrid. "I'm honored to hear such things, Lady Astrid."

Not for the first time, Astrid marked the gleam in his smoke-grey eyes when he fixed his gaze upon her. Malcolm was six years her junior, yet the force of his character made him seem older.

Heat washed over Astrid then, her old shyness threatening to shatter her composure. Aye, she could play the game, yet flirting would never come easily to her. However, while she'd waited in her bedchamber earlier, she decided that a little flattery aimed in the right direction could help her cause.

Astrid inclined her head in response. "Of course, I'd be interested to see just how *much* skill ye have with a blade," she murmured. The skin of her chest started to prickle, and she willed herself not to blush.

A cough intruded then, and her gaze shifted across the table to where Finn appeared to have swallowed something the wrong way. The marshal thumped him on the back, but Finn paid him little mind. His eyes were narrowed as they fixed upon her.

Ignoring him, Astrid shifted her attention back to Malcolm, who was grinning now. He was loving the attention.

"Ye are a charming lass," Tormod said then, amusement lacing his voice. "But we all know ye aren't here to flirt with my son ... but for an answer."

Astrid's embarrassment cooled at these words, relief sweeping over her. She wasn't sure how much longer she could flatter Malcolm. Determination clenched in her belly as she met the clan-chief's gaze once more. Finally, they'd returned to the reason she was here. "Aye," she admitted. "Do ye have one for me?"

19: THE LAST WORD

TORMOD HELD HER gaze for a few moments before his lips quirked. "Ye have fire in yer belly, Lady Astrid ... something I like in a woman."

Astrid didn't reply. Instead, she waited for the clan-chief's response.

So much rested upon it.

"Very well," he said eventually, lifting his pewter goblet to his lips and taking a sip. "The Macleods of Dunvegan will rally on yer behalf."

Astrid's heart kicked hard against her ribs, although she throttled the urge to grin and whoop. "Thank ye, Tormod," she replied, bowing her head. Lord, she'd been ready for him to deny her, and for a fraught exchange to ensue. What a relief that he wouldn't fight her on this. The tension that had been building within her since their arrival here dissolved. Now they just had to get back to Loch fast.

"I'll provide three galleys," Tormod went on.

Astrid's elation dimmed. She'd hoped for a larger fleet than that.

"We are facing a combined force of Mackinnons, MacGregors, and MacNabs," Finn spoke up then, his voice sharp. "*Three* birlinns won't be enough."

Astrid tensed, irritation spearing through her. Curse it, the man's bluntness was like a mallet between the eyes. Why couldn't he leave this to her?

Tormod's mouth pursed while beside him Malcolm's smile had faded.

"If I give ye too many galleys, I will leave my castle undefended," the clan-chief replied after a pause, his gaze settling upon Finn. "We have our own enemies. The MacDonalds of Duntulm are forever baying at our borders these days ... and the Mackinnons of Dunan are a thorn in my arse. I'll not make myself vulnerable to any of them."

"*Five* birlinns wouldn't do that, surely?" Astrid asked, deliberately softening her voice to compensate for Finn's brusqueness.

Tormod frowned.

Meanwhile, Malcolm's brow also furrowed. "Ye know the storm that brought ye to grief also destroyed two of our birlinns?"

Astrid nodded, her gaze meeting Malcolm's then. "I understand what I'm asking, Malcolm," she replied. "And I wouldn't ask unless our need was dire."

The clan-chief's son stared back at her, his smoke-grey eyes darkening to slate. His expression softened then, his brow smoothing.

Meanwhile, Tormod cleared his throat, drawing Astrid's attention once more. "My son doesn't decide such things," he said, irritation lacing his voice now. "*I* do."

Astrid tensed, realizing her mistake. He might be getting on in age, but Tormod wasn't yet ready to relinquish the reins of power. "Apologies," she replied, deliberately holding his gaze rather than lowering it. There was little point in feigning meekness with this man. "But I fear we may already be too late."

"We might be." Moments passed, and then Tormod sighed, leaning back in his carven chair. The great seat dwarfed his emaciated body, yet there was still a strength about him as he drummed the gnarled fingers of his right hand on the armrest. "Yet three galleys are all ye are getting, Lady Astrid," he said finally, glancing at his son then before they shared a long look. "Malcolm will lead them."

Astrid's throat tightened at these words, yet she kept her disappointment leashed. Meanwhile, Finn's face had gone taut.

There was an edge of steel in the Macleod's tone, warning both of them to insist at their peril.

But three birlinns were better than nothing. Malcolm had boasted earlier that the Macleod fleet had at least two forty-oar galleys too. With the Macleods on their side, all wasn't lost.

Malcolm rose to his feet then, his voice cutting through the rumble of conversation below the dais. "We're going to war, lads," he shouted to them. Surprised faces turned to him before the laird's son continued, "The Macleans of Mull have called for help, and we shall answer. And ye'll be pleased to hear ... we'll be crossing swords with the *Mackinnons* this time!"

A blood-thirsty roar followed this admission, and Astrid's skin prickled.

"Get yer arses up, and ready yerselves," Malcolm boomed then. "We sail at first light tomorrow!"

Taking a large gulp of wine, Astrid glanced down at her goblet. It was nearly empty. She'd drunk more than she was used to. The evening was drawing out, and the great hall had emptied, leaving just the clan-chief's table and the minstrels playing in the gallery above.

Meanwhile, Finn had moved up the table so that he sat next to the clan-chief. He and Tormod now discussed the resources the Macleans had at their disposal. The old man peppered him with questions, and Finn answered all of them confidently. He knew the Maclean's defenses well.

But so did Astrid, and irritation coiled inside her as the men's conversation drew out. She didn't appreciate being ignored.

"Ye'll be pleased to hear that preparations are well under way, Lady Astrid."

Astrid glanced up to see Malcolm striding across the rush-strewn floor toward her, a grin upon his face. The clan-chief's son had departed the hall for a spell, to oversee his men readying for departure, but he returned now and approached the dais. Dropping onto the bench-seat next to Astrid, he reached out and poured himself a large tankard of ale.

Astrid smiled back, even if she was aware of how close he was now sitting. Malcolm had slid along the bench so that their thighs were touching. She wanted to inch away from him yet was wary of giving offense. "That's a relief."

"Here ... have some more wine," he said, reaching for the nearby ewer.

Astrid shook her head and placed a hand over her goblet. She'd had enough and didn't wish to muddle her wits. "Thank ye, but wine gives me a sore head," she lied.

Malcolm nodded, even as his gaze boldly traveled over her face, his expression sobering. And as his stare drew out, a hungry look ignited in his eyes.

His interest in her earlier had been evident enough, but there was an aggressive edge to it now. Malcolm Macleod was a young man used to getting what he wanted.

Astrid's breathing became shallow, nervousness tightening her ribs. Curse it, what had she gotten herself into? She'd thought that flattering Malcolm a little and saying a few things to make pride swell in his chest would encourage him to help her.

However, she'd given him the impression she was interested in being wooed by him—when she wasn't.

"Malcolm," Tormod interrupted them, his tone sharp now. "Instead of making calf eyes at Lady Astrid, why don't ye listen in? Captain MacDonald has news about the defenses at Dounarwyse."

Malcolm tensed, irritation flashing across his face. A faint flush stained his cheekbones as he turned and focused his attention on Tormod and Finn. "Of course," he replied, a sullen edge creeping into his voice.

Tormod shifted his focus back to Finn. "Ye were saying, MacDonald."

"The Macleans of Dounarwyse have built earthworks along their northern boundary," Finn replied. A groove had etched between his eyebrows as he spoke, and his gaze settled upon Astrid for the first time since he'd begun conversing with the clan-chief. Astrid spied censure in his eyes.

Irritation speared her then. What right did he have to give her such a look? She hadn't done anything wrong.

"Aye ... but will it hold back the Mackinnons?" Malcolm asked.

"For a spell ... the banks are twenty feet high with ditches and spikes on the northern side," Finn answered. "Kendric Mackinnon will have seen the earthworks though ... and that's perhaps why he's chosen to attack from the sea."

"So, ye have a combined force of around two hundred warriors, ye say?" Tormod's bushy white eyebrows drew together as he regarded Finn. "I can see why ye need our help. Earthworks and sturdy walls will only protect ye up to a point ... they're no substitute for steel."

"Under normal circumstances, it would be a decent enough army," Astrid cut in, annoyed that the men continued to leave her out of the conversation. Her gaze speared the clan-chief's. "But this isn't a mere skirmish ... Kendric Mackinnon intends to *destroy* my clan."

A brittle silence followed these ominous words. It was a dramatic thing to say, yet it was the truth, and Astrid wanted to make the situation clear for the Macleods.

Malcolm was the first to recover. Flashing her a confident smile, he reached out and placed a large hand over hers. "Not to worry, lass ... *we'll* ensure they don't. Leave it to us to beat those Mackinnons into submission."

"Well ... that could have gone better," Finn announced as he followed Astrid into the chamber. He then kicked the door shut behind them.

Astrid snorted, turning to face Finn. "It could have gone far *worse* ... as ye well know. We should be celebrating that Tormod has agreed to help us ... I feared the worst."

He pulled a face. "Aye ... but three birlinns likely won't be enough to crush the Mackinnons."

Astrid frowned, folding her arms across her chest. She was aware of that; she didn't need him rubbing her face in it. "Ye were supposed to let *me* conduct the negotiations," she pointed out, her tone clipped.

Finn halted in front of her, his mouth thinning. "I'm not one to sit there and nod like a fool."

"No one asked ye to play the idiot," Astrid countered. "But the Macleod has to be handled carefully." A muscle flexed in Finn's jaw, yet she ignored his reaction. "If ye throw Tormod's generosity back in his face, ye risk him withdrawing his support."

"That's not what I was doing." Finn stepped closer then, and she inhaled his scent, leather and pine blended with the clean smell of his skin. Like her, he wore fresh clothes. Rather than donning his usual leathers, he'd been provided with dark-brown braies and a cream-colored lèine, which he wore open at the throat. "A man like Tormod sees capitulation as weakness. I had to challenge him."

Heat washed over Astrid. *Weakness.* The word cut her to the bone as if he'd suddenly unmasked her.

"I was about to *challenge* him," she ground out. "Until ye barged in like a ram at a gate. If ye'd let me, I might have persuaded him to give us the extra birlinns."

"I think not," he shot back. "The old man is intractable. Ye've got a persuasive tongue, lass ... but even *ye* have yer limits."

Astrid's temper spiked, and she shifted nearer to him. His sarcasm goaded her beyond her limits. "Well, we'll never know now, will we?"

"There ye go again." Finn's mouth twisted, his gaze never leaving hers. "Always with the last word."

20: LUST AND LOATHING

ASTRID TOOK A slow, steadying breath. Lord, the man was vexing. How she wanted to slap him, yet her father had always told her that raising one's fists when a discussion turned heated was a sign of poor wits—a sign someone was out of their depth.

But the truth was that she *was* out of her depth.

She hadn't gotten all the support Loch needed. She knew it, and so did Finn.

And he'd never let her forget it.

"Loch made a mistake sending ye with me," she said, her fists balling at her sides. "I need someone who'll *support* me in meetings, not undermine me."

"God's troth, ye'd test the patience of a saint." His eyes glinted green with sudden anger. "There isn't a man in Scotland with the fortitude to suffer ye, woman!"

A red veil dropped over her gaze at this insult, and without thinking, she shoved him hard in the chest. "Cur!"

Finn's hands snapped up, and he caught her by the wrists. Then, instead of answering her insult, as she'd expected, he pulled her against him.

An instant later, his mouth collided with hers.

The suddenness of the move surprised Astrid, and she gasped. Finn answered with a groan, his tongue sweeping her lips apart.

Their kiss on the beach earlier that day, when they'd spied the ship approaching, had been thrilling—but right from the first moments, this one was different. It was hot and demanding, almost as if Finn was issuing her a challenge.

Ever since that first kiss, tension had been building between them—their argument now had merely stoked a fire that neither of them wished to acknowledge.

And it shocked Astrid to the core that she answered him without hesitation. Her lips grazed his lips, her tongue stroking his.

The kiss quickly grew wild.

Another groan rumbled in Finn's throat, and he hauled her closer still. Earlier, a maid had helped Astrid dress, and brushed her hair with a hog-bristle brush before pinning half of it up and letting the other half tumble down her back.

Finn deftly removed the pins now, and they pinged as they hit the floor. He then carded his fingers through her hair, gently entwining his hands in it. Meanwhile, Astrid's hands slid up his chest to where his lèine parted at the throat. Lord, his skin was so hot, and his body pressed against hers was deliciously hard. Finn's nearness made her senses reel. The feel of his mouth devouring hers, and the taste of him, made her belly dip and soar as if she were on a swing.

However, as the kiss drew out, and need pulsed between them, Astrid tried to claw back her wits.

Hades, what was she doing? She was tangling tongues with her enemy, for pity's sake. This couldn't go on.

Leaning back, she tore her mouth from his, breathing hard as their gazes met once more.

"Wait," she gasped. "I hate ye, *remember*?"

"No, ye don't," he growled. Lord, she wished he wouldn't look at her like that. The heat of his stare made her feel as if she were melting.

"But ye still loathe *me*, don't ye?"

"No." He cupped her face with his hands, his lips finding hers once more. This kiss was deep and sensual, and within moments, Astrid was drowning in him. Her tongue dueled with his in a lusty dance that turned her lower belly molten.

A heartbeat later, she was entwined in his arms once more, their bodies pressed hard against each other.

And then she felt it—something long and hard that thrust against her belly.

Although she was a maid, and had no experience at all of this, Astrid realized that he was aroused. Aye, she'd heard the servants at Duart whisper about such things over the years. Even through the layers of clothing separating them, she could feel his erection, and without questioning her behavior, she found herself going up on tiptoe and grinding her pelvis against his, attempting to bring that burning shaft closer to where she now ached to be touched.

Finn ripped his mouth from hers then, burying it in her neck. Breathing hard, he licked and kissed his way down. Shuddering with pleasure, Astrid let her head fall back, a soft moan escaping her as his tongue slid into the hollow between her collar bones and down the shallow valley beneath it.

Cool air feathered against her skin then, and she half-opened her eyes to see that he'd slid her lowcut surcote, kirtle, and the lèine she wore underneath, off her shoulders.

Her breasts were naked and bared to him.

"Beautiful," Finn murmured huskily, lowering himself before her.

Astrid's chest heaved, thrusting her peaked nipples in his face. An instant later, his hungry mouth fastened upon a swollen tip, and he gently began to suckle her.

Pleasure darted straight to Astrid's core. Biting her lip, she slid her hands into Finn's hair. Its texture was fine and silky, yet thick, and she delighted in stroking it as he suckled one breast hungrily and then the other.

After a while though, it was difficult to focus on anything except his mouth, and his ministrations roughened, his teeth gently grazing her nipples.

Astrid whimpered and pushed herself against him, even as the flesh between her thighs ached and pulsed in time with her heartbeat. She'd never felt so needy, so wanting.

Eventually, Finn rose to his feet, hauling her into his arms again for another wild kiss. And as their lips, teeth, and tongues tangled, he walked her across the chamber to where a wooden chair with a high back and carved armrests sat next to the glowing hearth.

His mouth still plundering hers, Finn pushed her down onto the chair before lowering himself to his knees before her once more.

"What are ye doing?" High and breathy, Astrid's voice didn't sound like her own.

Finn's gaze ensnared hers. She'd never seen his face like this. His skin was taut, stretched tight over his cheekbones, while his mouth was swollen from their kisses, and his hazel eyes had deepened to green in the firelight.

"I'd like nothing more than to take ye to bed, lass," he said, a rasp to his voice, "and swive ye until dawn." Heat flushed over Astrid at these bold words, yet Finn hadn't finished. "But I'll not ruin ye."

Astrid's lips parted as the urge to tell him he could ruin her if he wanted rose up. Grasping onto her sanity, she choked back the words.

Finn was right. She was a clan-chief's sister, and although she'd made it clear to Loch that she wouldn't wed anyone against her will, she knew what price her maidenhead had to a prospective husband.

Even so, disappointment welled within her. How she wanted to see Finn naked, to explore his skin with her fingertips, lips, and tongue. She longed to see his shaft too, for she'd only glimpsed it that day in the cave, and since he'd been freezing, his manhood had tucked itself away in the sparse nest of hazel-colored hair between his thighs.

"Ye wish to stop?" Her voice caught then, betraying her disappointment.

His mouth quirked, even as his gaze burned into her. "Not before I give ye the pleasure ye deserve."

Astrid stared back at him, not understanding.

Finn's lips curved again as he reached down and took hold of the hem of her skirts. He then pushed them up, revealing her bare legs. And then, before she knew what he was doing, Finn had spread her thighs wide, hooking each over the armrests of the chair, and settled himself between her legs.

Astrid stopped breathing.

21: BY A THREAD

FINN HAD OPENED her up in such a vulnerable position that heat now prickled Astrid's skin, a flush sweeping up from her belly to her chest, throat, and cheeks.

This was indecent—as was the way he now stared at what lay between her parted thighs—yet there was a wicked part of her that welcomed the impropriety.

The look on Finn's face right now was almost feral. His lips were parted, and he was breathing hard as if he'd been running. However, she caught a glimmer of tenderness in his eyes as well, and it made her trust him.

Trust him?

Aye, somehow, over the past days, her attitude toward him had changed. His revelation about Maggie had confused her—and she was still confused—yet their kiss on the beach had revealed that, underneath the loathing, she was wildly attracted to him.

An attraction that shivered in the air every time their gazes met afterward.

However, Astrid had no more time to dwell on the significance of what they were doing, or the reasons for it, for Finn lowered his face between her thighs and licked her—right *there*.

Astrid gasped, both scandalized and thrilled by his act. She must have been living under a rock her whole life, for she'd had no idea that lovers did such things to each other. She certainly hadn't heard servants whispering about *this*.

Finn licked her again before he dove in, devouring her sex with a single-minded determination that made Astrid jolt and shudder with shock.

An instant later, delicious pleasure began to throb and pulse where his tongue and lips worked. Astrid let her head fall back against the chair, her eyes fluttering shut.

The Saints forgive her, she'd had no idea it was possible to feel this good.

She started to tremble then, while Finn continued, relentless. The moments slid by, and tension began to gather in the cradle of her hips, coiling and drawing tight, as if she was edging toward something.

His tongue flicked a sensitive spot nestled within the petals of her sex, and Astrid's body jerked of its own accord. Her eyes snapped open, and she curved forward, her gaze lowering to where he still devoured her.

"Oh, God," she gasped, as a tide rose inside her. "What are ye doing?"

Finn didn't respond. She wasn't even sure he'd heard her, for his attention was wholly focused between her thighs.

Watching him tipped her over the brink. Her trembling deepened into a full-body shudder, a reaction she couldn't seem to stop. Finn focused on that tender pearl of flesh between her thighs, his tongue swirling and flicking until Astrid unraveled.

Waves of ecstasy thrummed through her loins, making her writhe and buck against his mouth. And all the while, Finn kept up his sensual torture, wringing every last sobbed gasp out of her.

In the aftermath, Astrid collapsed, sweaty and panting in the chair. Her body felt like a puddle of melted tallow. Even if she wanted to, she couldn't have stood up.

Breathing hard too, Finn rocked back on his heels.

Astrid's gaze slid down from his flushed face, over his heaving chest, to where a large erection now tented his braies. A damp patch had appeared there, spreading as she watched it.

A rush of wet heat pulsed deep in her womb at the sight of his excitement.

Glancing down, following her gaze, Finn grimaced. "I should have realized that might happen," he rasped.

"Let me help ye," Astrid whispered, pushing herself up from where she'd sagged in the chair. She reached for him then, desperate to unlace his braies and see his engorged, leaking rod for herself. However, to her surprise, Finn shook his head and moved back, out of reach.

"No, lass," he said huskily. "Once ye start touching me there, the self-control that I'm hanging onto by a thread will snap ... and the next thing will be that I'm buried to the hilt inside ye." He cleared his throat then. "I will *not* ruin ye."

Another rush of wild need pulsed through Astrid's core. Hades, she knew she was being a reckless fool, yet she wanted nothing else than to see Finn's self-restraint shatter. She wanted to be thoroughly *ruined*.

Nonetheless, he'd said no, and she sensed that to push things would be folly.

And so, she shakily pushed down her skirts and hauled herself upright in the chair, trying to ignore her craving for him and the gentle throb in her womb.

The fog of lust that had addled her wits was clearing now, and she understood the wisdom of his words. They had to stop before things spiraled out of control.

Finn pushed himself off the floor and rose to his feet above her.

Trying not to stare at his groin, Astrid looked up at him. Her chest constricted then when she glimpsed the stricken look in his eyes. Tension vibrated off his lean frame as he moved away from her and walked stiffly toward the door that separated their chambers.

"Bar the door between our rooms tonight, Astrid," he ordered roughly. "And I shall see ye at dawn."

Stepping into his chamber, Finn pushed the door closed and sagged against it.

His heart was pounding so hard that dizziness closed in on him and nausea bit his throat.

His body, his very soul, cried out to return to that chamber.

Christ, how he wanted Astrid Maclean on her knees in front of him, greedily sucking his rod. How he wanted her naked on her back while he plowed her senseless, their bodies slick with sweat. He wanted to hear her cries echo high into the rafters. He wanted to lose himself in her.

He'd never yearned for anything more.

And yet he would not, could not.

It wasn't just a matter of taking her maidenhead either. Finn wasn't that noble—Astrid was willing, and he wasn't made of stone. No, that was an easy excuse, but it wasn't the real reason he'd pulled back.

While he was pleasuring her, he remained in control. Even so, he'd been on the brink of losing it when she reached for him.

But he couldn't let his façade crumble. The indifference he'd cloaked himself in over the years was an old friend, and he didn't want to shed it.

His survival depended on it.

Vulnerability was for fools.

His parents had taught him that. Maggie had taught him that. And Astrid herself had done so too.

Accompanying Astrid on this mission had been folly from the beginning. They'd spent too much time together—and somehow, he'd gone from hating the woman to wanting her again.

Only now, he wasn't a callow youth.

These days, he kept himself emotionally distant from others, and that was the way he liked it.

Lifting a hand to his face, Finn saw it was shaking. *Shite.* He was a mess, and his cods were still throbbing piteously. He glanced down, his mouth thinning as he viewed the wet patch at his groin. The wood in his braies still hadn't subsided.

Aye, his self-control astounded him. A weaker man would be bollocks deep inside Astrid right now.

Finn clenched his jaw. He didn't feel like a hero though— quite the opposite.

22: A TRANSGRESSION

DAMP AIR WHISPERED against Astrid's face as she hurried along the jetty to where one of the three birlinns Tormod Macleod had promised awaited. Nervous excitement fluttered under her ribcage.

Finally, they were heading back to Mull. Her brother would soon have reinforcements. She just hoped they wouldn't be too late.

Farther out, at the mouth to the inlet that led out into Dunvegan Loch, two other galleys had dropped anchor. Running a critical eye over them, Astrid's gaze narrowed.

She'd expected the clan-chief to at least provide the biggest birlinns he had. However, all the galleys she could see were sixteen-oar craft. With two men per oar, this meant that the Macleod's force would be around ninety-six warriors.

Her breathing quickened. It was a decent enough force, but would it be enough to turn the tide against the Mackinnons?

It has to be. Astrid took a deep breath and marched down the jetty to where a tall, muscular young man with wild auburn hair, a fur cloak hanging from his broad shoulders, had stepped off the birlinn. Behind the clan-chief's son, the other warriors laughed and ribbed each other, the mood merry despite the early hour.

Malcolm flashed her a wide grin. "Good morning, Lady Astrid."

"Good morning," she greeted him with a tight smile.

Malcolm's gaze then shifted behind her before he nodded. "Captain MacDonald."

"Morning," Finn replied gruffly.

Astrid tensed. Hades, how awkward it was now.

She'd slept poorly that night, images of what they'd done returning to torment her as the hours slid by. Her breathing had turned ragged as she'd imagined what would have happened had Finn not stopped things. Aye, she was a virgin, yet she'd seen animals couple and knew how bairns were made.

She knew what Finn would do with that impressive swelling within his braies.

But as her fantasies expanded, growing in full, shocking detail, she'd grown restless and sweaty—and confused.

When the first light peeked through the sacking covering the tiny window, Astrid had already washed and dressed. She'd then lifted the bar to the door that separated their chambers and waited for Finn to appear.

He'd done so presently, dressed in his leathers and armed, his heavy fur-lined cloak swinging from his shoulders. However, his expression was shuttered when he looked her way. "Ready to go?" he'd asked, his tone terse.

Astrid had nodded, even as her skin prickled with embarrassment.

Was this how it was to be between them now? Were they to return to barely tolerating each other, to pretending last night hadn't happened?

But it had, and as she stood upon the jetty with the dawn sun kissing her face and the solid walls of Dunvegan Castle rearing above her, Astrid remembered how Finn had pleasured her. Her stomach did a little flip then, her breath catching.

Curse her, she couldn't ever think of him in the same way again. Finn wasn't standing overly close to her now, yet with every step she'd taken as they wound their way down from the sea gate, she'd been keenly aware of his presence.

At some point—once they had privacy—they'd have to speak about what happened.

"Best we get away," Malcolm informed them, jerking his chin toward the eddying water. "The tide is turning."

Astrid nodded and approached the clan-chief's son, allowing him to help her into the galley nearest. Enough worrying about Finn; she needed to focus on reaching Dounarwyse fast—and on what would happen when they did.

"Seat yerself at the bow, Lady Astrid," Malcolm instructed. "MacDonald, take a seat next to Errol" —he gestured to the space next to one of the oarsmen— "and ready yerself to row."

Doing as bid, Astrid perched on a narrow plank near the bow.

But as she put a hand out to grip the railing, fear grasped her by the throat. Suddenly, she was back in the midst of that awful storm, clinging for dear life as waves the size of mountains rose above her. The awful sound of the galley breaking up, the mast and rigging snapping, ripped through her then, as did a vision of the square sail billowing as it kissed the water.

Blind panic surged through Astrid, and she lurched to her feet so quickly that she nearly lost her balance.

A hand shot out, gripping her arm to steady her.

An instant later, Astrid's gaze met Finn's.

He'd just stepped onto the birlinn and was now so close that she could see the flecks of green in his hazel eyes. "Easy, Astrid," he murmured. "It's safe."

"Is it?" Her voice caught as terror gripped her by the throat once more. "Or will we come to grief again ... and meet a watery end like the rest of our crew?"

Tension rippled across Finn's face. "It was a freak storm, lass," he replied, his voice still low so that the warriors seated at the oars behind them wouldn't overhear. "If the sea was that wild usually, no one would ever set sail."

Astrid stared back at him, fear still beating hysterically against her ribs. She wanted to believe him, yet the memories were all so fresh—and stepping back on this birlinn brought everything to the fore.

Tears pricked her eyelids then, and she swallowed hard.

Weak woman, she inwardly raged at herself, as she spied Malcolm looking her way. *Now isn't the time to crumble.*

"Astrid?"

She snapped out of her reverie to find Finn's brow furrowed, worry shadowing his eyes. "Are ye well?"

Swallowing once more, Astrid nodded. She wasn't, yet she'd do her best to keep herself together.

Loch is relying on me. My clan is relying on me. She repeated the words in her head as she lowered herself to her seat once more. *I can't let them down.*

The reminder helped, and she managed to push herself back from teetering on the edge of panic.

Satisfied that she wasn't going to try and scramble off the birlinn and flee back to the castle, Finn moved on, settling himself next to Errol, while Malcolm unmoored the galley.

Astrid dragged in a long, slow breath before letting it out gently through her nose. Steadying her breathing helped, and although her panic and fear still simmered, she stayed put while the men used their oars to push the birlinn out through the shallow inlet toward the loch.

Reaching down, her fingers traced absently over the two belts she'd strapped on at her waist. Her dirk and her set of throwing knives. She'd had them cleaned and sharpened the previous afternoon, fearing that the salt water might rust or dull the edges. Wearing the weapons should have bolstered her confidence, yet steel was no match for the wrath of the sea.

No match for the darkness that crowded in whenever a crisis loomed.

Arming yerself thus and having the skill to throw knives and wield a dagger is all well and good, lass, a cruel voice whispered to her then. *But what will happen when yer life is in danger and ye must take a man's life with one of the blades ye carry? What then? Will ye lose yer wits as ye almost did just now?*

Sanna brought back painful memories of the crew they'd lost.

As Finn trudged up the beach, to where the Macleod force was making camp above the tideline, he glanced up at the cluster of crofts perched on the lush green hillside.

He was relieved they weren't staying in the hamlet—not that it could accommodate their band anyway. Even alighting upon the beach made him remember how Dougie had tripped over while they were hauling the *Sea Eagle* onto the sand, and how the other lads had ribbed him. He recalled each of their faces as they sat around the fire in the barn that eve—Norris's eagerness and Roy's teasing when they'd played knucklebones. Dougie had been so proud of his newly honed skills at knucklebones, and now the young warrior was dead.

An ache rose under his breastbone, and absently, Finn patted the pouch he still carried at his belt. He hadn't touched the knucklebones since that evening. Usually, when making camp with other warriors like this, he'd rally a group of them for a game once they settled in for the evening. However, today, he didn't have the stomach for it.

Not when the grief was still so raw.

Instead, he joined the men who were putting up the largest of the two hide tents—one for Malcolm Macleod and the other for Astrid Maclean. Everyone else, Finn included, would sleep under the stars.

Finn glanced around him then, looking for Astrid.

He spied her on the beach, with a handful of men, as they scoured the sand for driftwood to fuel the fires overnight. She'd already collected an armload and was making her way back up to the camp.

Even though he knew he shouldn't, Finn tracked her with his gaze. She walked with a straight back, her chin held high. He'd seen her falter that morning though after she'd boarded the birlinn. He'd been loath to set sail again on a birlinn too, for the memories were all very fresh. Alec Rankin's cog had been different, somehow. The vessel was larger for one thing, and it was taking them away from the isle where they'd been stranded. But this galley brought the terror, the loss, back.

Finn had kept a close eye on Astrid as they departed, worried that panic might overtake her, yet she'd kept her nerve.

He averted his attention then, lest she catch him looking. The woman was full of contradictions—and her response to him the night before had been another surprise.

She'd kissed him with hunger, had been eager for his touch, and exquisitely responsive.

Heat kindled in his gut as he recalled how she'd shattered against his tongue. He couldn't touch her like that again, but he'd never forget what they'd shared.

Reining in his wayward thoughts, Finn surveyed the men surrounding him. This evening, their moods were subdued, their gazes inward. Battle was on the horizon. It would take them most of the following day to reach Mull, yet reach it they would. And when they did, no one knew what awaited them.

Finn picked up a wooden stake and drove it into the soft sand, his mouth thinning. By the time they returned to Mull, they'd have been away six days.

Anything could have happened in the meantime.

The Mackinnons could have destroyed Dounarwyse's defenses.

Kendric Mackinnon could now be the new laird of the broch.

Scowling, Finn tried to banish the worries. Nonetheless, as soon as he did, new ones crept in.

23: I MISJUDGED YE

"ARE YE NOT hungry, Lady Astrid?"

Glancing up from where she'd been gazing down at the bread, cheese, and dried sausage on her lap, Astrid met Malcolm's eye. They were seated in front of a fire upon the beach, the ruddy flames and sprays of sparks kissing the night.

As always, the young warrior watched her with keen interest—far too much interest, in fact.

"I'm not a big eater," she replied with a shrug. That was true enough, although after a day at sea, breathing in the fresh sea air, she should have been famished. However, worry about what was happening on Mull had robbed her of appetite.

"Ye should eat more," Malcolm said, raising an auburn eyebrow. "No man wants a lass who's as tiny as a sparrow."

Astrid stiffened, her face warming. "Do ye speak for all men then, Malcolm?" she said, her tone clipped now. "I thought their tastes vary, as do women's."

She, for one, preferred men with more manners.

Malcolm snorted as if the very idea was preposterous. "Aye, well … tastes aside, a lass has to be sturdy enough to carry a bairn, at least. Ye look as if giving birth would rip ye asunder."

An awkward silence fell then, and heat bloomed across Astrid's face. "Slender women can carry bairns as well as any other," she ground out finally, anger rising under her embarrassment. "And believe it or not, a woman has a worth beyond swiving and producing bairns."

Malcolm's smirk dissolved, his grey eyes snapping wide. Across the fire, Finn wore a slight, smug, smile.

She expected the clan-chief's son to make a scathing reply to that, yet he now looked as if he'd swallowed his tongue. Silence fell at their fire once more, while around them, the rumble of men's voices traveled down the beach, punctuated by the odd burst of laughter. The sea of individual hearths lit up the night like glowing fireflies.

"Ye told us last night about the defenses around Dounarwyse ... but does the fortress have any weaknesses we don't know about?" Malcolm asked eventually, his voice a touch surly.

Astrid's brow furrowed at this question, her already tense stomach twisting tight. For once, she didn't know how to answer, and she glanced over at Finn, hoping he did.

His smile slipped, a frown replacing it. "The broch itself would be hard to breach," he admitted hesitantly. "It sits upon a steep motte and has high walls that will be difficult to scale." He paused then, his frown deepening. "Its weakness, I suppose, is that it can be approached with relative ease from both land and sea."

"That'll also work in *our* favor," Malcolm reminded him.

"True enough." Finn brushed the crumbs of his supper off his lap. Unlike Astrid, he'd wolfed his meal down. "I just hope the Mackinnon fleet hasn't made short work of our sea defenses in the meantime."

Astrid's breathing grew shallow. That was her fear too. The battle might well be over. Her brother might be dead.

With difficulty, she pushed the chilling thought aside.

No, she wouldn't entertain the possibility. She had to believe that Dounarwyse's defenses had held and that Loch was still fighting.

"And what of Kendric Mackinnon's battle style?" Malcolm's brow furrowed. "Is he an aggressor or one to draw his enemy close before striking?"

"Both, when needs be," Finn replied. "I've only fought in one skirmish against the Mackinnons ... years ago now, before I left Mull to follow The Bruce. The Mackinnons were sly on that occasion, waiting to ambush a group of us patrolling our northern borders."

"Aye, he earned his name, 'The Butcher of Dùn Ara'," Astrid pointed out. "Mackinnon is ruthless, vicious, and cleverer than a fox." She paused then, the back of her nape prickling. "And he's incensed too ... which makes him even more dangerous."

Malcolm's mouth pursed. "His rage may be his weakness too though," he pointed out.

"Aye," Finn murmured. "Vengeance has a way of addling a man's wits."

Astrid nodded, in full agreement with them both. They'd both seen what a lust for revenge had done to Loch's cousin. Jack had slid into a kind of madness until Tara had pulled him free. "This attack, although not unexpected, is bold." She paused then, her mind working. "And his alliance with the MacGregors and MacNabs is new, untested. If we come in aggressively tomorrow, it might be enough to make them waver. They'll be exhausted, after days of fighting, after all ... but we won't be."

"*We?*" Finn asked, a challenge in his voice. "*Ye* won't be going anywhere near the battle, Astrid."

Astrid stilled, heat flooding over. "I *have* to be there," she replied, cutting Finn a baleful look.

"No, ye don't," he shot back.

Malcolm cleared his throat. "Back to the Mackinnons," he said pointedly. "I suggest that we don't announce our arrival."

"Aye, the element of surprise is our greatest ally," Finn agreed.

Astrid's brow furrowed. "How will we discern friend from foe?"

The clan-chief's son flashed her a reckless grin. "Do ye want me to ask before I stick my dirk into anyone, lass?"

Astrid frowned. She wasn't in the mood to be teased, and didn't like not knowing what lay ahead either. She wished they could have sent a scout ahead to bring word back on the situation, yet they had neither the time nor the resources. As such, they'd go in blind.

Fatigue pressed down upon her then. She'd slept little the night before and was now desperate for rest. She had to be fresh for the dawn.

Wrapping up the remains of her supper in an oiled cloth, for she'd try to eat the rest in the morning, Astrid rose to her feet.

Her tent was just a few yards distant, and she longed to stretch out on a sheepskin. However, her attention shifted to Finn.

They'd barely spoken directly all day, and apart from their exchange first thing when she'd panicked upon stepping onto the birlinn, their interactions had been formal, stilted.

It was awkward, and as their gazes met now, something twisted deep in Astrid's chest.

No, she couldn't retire for the eve quite yet.

"MacDonald," she said, deliberately keeping her voice neutral with Malcolm looking on. "Can I have a word ... in private?"

Finn's shoulders tensed at the request. But after a moment, he unfolded his long body and rose to his feet. Nodding to Malcolm, who was watching them both closely, he moved toward Astrid.

Without another word, she turned and walked away, leading him down the beach, to where no one would be able to overhear them. As she walked, Astrid squared her shoulders and steeled herself.

There was unfinished business between them, and she couldn't go into battle tomorrow without speaking of it. Even so, her heart was now pounding like a hunting drum.

Once she was far enough away that the rumble of the surf drowned out the men's voices farther up the beach, she turned to Finn. He stopped a yard from her, his sharp-featured face frosted by moonlight, his gaze wary.

"What is it?" he asked tersely.

Astrid heaved in a deep breath and took a step closer to him. "Is this how we are to behave now, Finn?" She paused then, her throat tightening, before she forced herself on. "Are we to pretend that last night never happened?"

He stared back at her a moment before clearing his throat. "Aye."

God's teeth, her heart now felt as if it were about to explode from her breast. She wanted to flee from him, but her feet wouldn't move. "Why?"

A nerve flickered in his cheek. "It's easier that way."

Astrid's breathing caught, an ache rising under her ribs. "Perhaps ... but it would be a lie, wouldn't it?"

A beat of silence followed before Finn replied, a rasp in his voice. "I can't give ye what ye want, lass."

Astrid flinched as if he'd struck her. Heat flushed over her face then, and she was glad the night hid her embarrassment. "And what do ye b ... believe I want?" Lord, now she was stuttering like a fool.

His face went taut at this question. "Things I'm not prepared to give ... to anyone."

Silence fell between them, stretching out, before Astrid finally forced herself to answer. "I'm as s ... scared as ye are." Her voice faltered once more.

Aye, she was terrified, yet there had been too much left unsaid over the years. So much misunderstanding. At the very least, on the eve of battle, there would be honesty between them.

Finn reached up and dragged a hand down his face. His mouth then twisted. "I don't want to talk about this." The brittle edge to his voice made Astrid still. The man looked ready to bolt.

"I misjudged ye, Finn," she gasped out the words. "I understand now that ye weren't to blame for Maggie's death ... no one was. It was a tragic accident."

Astrid stopped abruptly, shocked by her admission. It wasn't a lie though. Initially, she'd denied his tale about Maggie, yet underneath, she'd known he'd told her the truth. "And I'm sorry for whipping the fishermen in Craignure into a frenzy after Maggie died ... and for every piece of hate that I have flung yer way over the years." She swallowed. "I wish I could take it all back."

Something that looked a bit like panic rippled over his face. "Then ye are a better person than me," he replied with a shake of his head. "If only I could cast aside the past ... but I can't."

"Why not?"

He remained stonily silent.

A sickly sensation washed over Astrid. She needed to let this be, but her tongue wouldn't still itself. "Speak to me, Finn ... let me in."

He shook his head, stubbornness filtering over his face.

"So, ye regret what happened between us?" Curse her, she wished her eyes weren't starting to prickle, that her throat didn't feel so tight. She was just moments away from weeping.

Finn stared back at her, a muscle feathering in his jaw. Silence swelled between them before he answered her, his voice low and rough. "Aye."

Astrid flinched.

Heart pounding, she stepped back from him and furiously tried to bank the tears that now stung her eyes. "At least ye are sincere," she managed, her voice choked. "I should thank ye for that."

"Astrid," he ground out. "Please, don't make this harder than it has to be. I can't—"

"Fear not," she cut him off as she continued to back away, mortification sweeping over her in a hot rush. "I shall not bring this up again."

Something gave way inside her then. She had to get away from him, had to gather what shreds of dignity she had left. Suddenly, she was fifteen summers old again, watching as the lad she pined for flirted with her best friend. His rejection ripped her asunder.

God help her, she thought she'd never be so foolish as to long for Finn MacDonald again, but she had.

Picking up her skirts with one hand and still clutching her parcel of food with the other, Astrid fled back up the beach toward the sanctuary of her tent.

24: NO PLACE FOR A LADY

"I WON'T BE a burden." Facing Malcolm and Finn on the beach, as the sun kissed the hills to the east, Astrid nodded to the warrior who'd just laced the bracer onto her forearm. The armguards fitted snugly. Once he moved away, she then patted the belt of blades at her hip. "These aren't for show ... I know how to use them."

Malcolm's eyes widened at this assertion, for this was the first time he'd seen Astrid wearing her throwing knives, although Finn's expression merely turned grim. Of course, he knew she wasn't lying. Nonetheless, her words didn't reassure him.

"I'll keep out of yer way, if that's what ye are worried about," she assured them as she put on a thick leather vest over the bodice of her kirtle and began to deftly lace it up. It was made of tough leather and would provide a little protection in battle.

Astrid was halfway through lacing herself up when she glanced over at Finn once more.

He was scowling at her. "I was more concerned about *yer safety* actually," he growled. "That vest won't prevent a pike from skewering ye."

"Well, then it's fortunate that I'm nimble and quick," she replied, raising her chin. "I'll ensure no schiltron finds its mark."

Her boast made Malcolm's mouth curve, although Finn's jaw now flexed. "Loch won't like it."

"Well, he's not here to voice his opinion, is he?"

Her words were deliberately flippant, and anger flickered to life in Finn's eyes. "Things will get brutal when we reach Dounarwyse." His voice roughened then. "Are ye ready to see blood gush from a man's throat, to see his entrails spill from his belly?"

The words were harsh, and Astrid's heart slammed hard against her ribs as she imagined such a scene.

However, she wouldn't back down. Over the past week, she'd been shipwrecked and marooned on a barren island, dealt with pirates, convinced a clan-chief against his will—and been humiliated by her lover. But she'd weathered it all. She was still standing. No, her spirit would prevail. It was time to step into the breach.

Finn would never know how his words the night before had wounded her. She'd not let on that she retreated to her tent and wept bitter tears, all the while railing at herself for succumbing to girlish fancies.

Where were her wits?

She'd made a stuttering fool of herself and misjudged Finn's attitude toward her, but she couldn't crawl away and hide.

Not from him. Not from anyone.

"Listen to me, Astrid." Finn moved close now. "Battle is no place for a lady. Malcolm has already agreed to make a detour south ... and to provide two of his men as an escort to ensure ye make it safely back to Duart."

"No!" Anger flared hot in Astrid's belly. How dare they discuss this without consulting her first? "There won't be time ... we risk being too late to help them as it is."

"Yer brother will be furious if we drag ye into the midst of a melee," Finn countered, bringing up Loch once more.

"MacDonald has raised some worthy points," Malcolm said then, folding his muscular arms across his chest. "Once we engage the enemy, things will get messy ... and bloody." He pulled a face. "I wouldn't want my sister thrust into the midst of a battle either."

"I repeat, I can fight," Astrid cut in.

"That's not enough." Finn's lean frame vibrated with anger now. "And although ye don't think ye'll be a burden, ye *will* be. Ye will also be a distraction ... something none of us need."

A chill silence fell then, and Astrid was aware of the stares of the men surrounding them. They were all waiting for the command to haul the birlinns into the water and resume their journey.

This argument was holding them up.

But Astrid wouldn't be moved. "Ye're not dropping me off, MacDonald." She bit out the words, enunciating each one carefully. "If ye want me to return to Duart, ye'll have to tie me up and drag me kicking and screaming back there yerself."

Moments passed, and then Malcolm cleared his throat. "Well, MacDonald … the lady has made her feelings plain." He paused then, his gaze flicking between where Finn and Astrid were glaring at each other. "And Lady Astrid is right … time is against us."

The dark smoke rising into the sky was an ill sign.

Sitting at the bow, Astrid narrowed her gaze, craning her neck forward to see into the distance.

Ahead, a smudge of green was visible. And as the moments passed, she realized she was looking at a windswept headland.

Her heart swooped. *Mull!*

The small fleet had cut across the water, a brisk wind filling their sails and pushing them on faster than expected. It was only mid-afternoon, yet the Isle of Mull was in sight.

However, the smoke that stained the blue sky throttled her joy.

Casting a glance over her shoulder, her gaze settled upon Finn's face. It was difficult to look his way, as she'd done her best to avoid him all day. Likewise, he hadn't spoken a word to her since their argument at dawn.

Fortunately, Finn wasn't focused on her at present. He'd moved up from amidships and was also staring southwest. "I hope that smoke isn't coming from the broch," he muttered, voicing her own fears.

"We'll see soon enough," Malcolm called from behind him. "Are ye ready for battle, lads?" His voice rose to a roar then, carrying across the water. And the cry that answered him was equally thunderous.

Astrid's skin prickled, her breathing growing shallow.

Hades, this was really happening. She was about to dive into the midst of chaos.

And as they sailed closer still, and the high walls of Dounarwyse became visible against the sky, her pulse sprang into a gallop.

At least her worst fears hadn't been realized—the broch hadn't already fallen. She remembered Loch saying that sieges could last a long while, as the attackers hurled themselves against the defenses before withdrawing, rallying themselves, and trying again.

Dounarwyse had never been an easy fortress to take, and it was proving so again now.

A sea of men swarmed around the base of the castle walls, and even from this distance, it looked as if they were taking a battering ram to the gate. Arrows and crossbow bolts flew from the ramparts. Dounarwyse's curtain wall had a battered look, with chunks of stone missing, and dark smears of soot, as if flaming projectiles had been hurled at the fortress. However, the smoke wasn't rising from the broch, at present, but from the water below.

And as they approached, Astrid's heart started to race so violently that it felt as if it would lurch from her chest. Another battle was unfolding upon the sea, and one of the birlinns, a large galley, was in flames. Men screamed and leaped into the water, while others remained onboard and still fired arrows at the cog that bore down upon them.

Astrid's breathing caught then, and she murmured an oath.

She recognized the cog with its distinctive black-and-white-striped sail.

Logan Black, the chieftain of Croggan, was here—which meant that the burning birlinn belonged to the attackers. That was a good sign indeed, one which took the edge off her mounting panic.

Keep yer wits about ye, woman, she counseled herself. *Ye asked for this. Now prove that ye will be a help, not a hindrance.*

Finn hadn't exaggerated. The fighting was brutal indeed. There was a tangle of birlinns that rocked precariously as men fought with pikes and dirks. Some fell into the water, yet they continued to flail at each other even then.

And as they drew nearer still, Astrid marked the dark-red patches that spread out across the water around the fighting, staining it.

"I'd say we're in time for the final battle," Malcolm announced. He'd moved up to the bow too, his auburn eyebrows knitted as he surveyed the melee.

"Aye," Finn agreed. "Although Astrid had a point yesterday ... it's going to be difficult to separate our allies from our enemies amongst this mess." He cut Malcolm a look then. "The cog is one of ours though."

Malcolm's attention shifted to the *Revenge Tide*, which, despite having set a foe's ship alight, was now beset by three other smaller birlinns. Men scrambled up, over the railings of the cog, and a violent skirmish was taking place on the deck. "Right," he murmured. "Then we shall begin there ... they look as if they could do with help."

He turned back to his men then. "Ready yerselves!" he bellowed. "We're defending the cog. Make sure ye are engaging a Mackinnon, MacGregor, or MacNab before ye drive yer blade into anyone's chest. Is that clear?"

"Aye!"

All three birlinns were sailing close now, in a tightly packed vee that reminded Astrid of a diving swallow.

"Astrid." Finn caught her arm then, focusing on her for the first time since their argument earlier in the day. His features were tight as he drew her up from her perch at the bow. "Ye're too vulnerable up here ... move to amidships and stay there."

The glint in his eyes warned that he wouldn't be argued with—not that Astrid intended to defy him. There were arrows and flaming projectiles hurtling around out there. As such, she gave a nod and turned, scrambling back, between where many of the warriors had abandoned their oars and were now drawing their weapons. The ring of steel, the rasp of iron against leather, filled the air.

And then, as Astrid drew the dirk at her hip and crouched next to the mast, they sailed into the midst of the sea battle, and the roar of men's voices, yells, and the clash of weapons filled the air.

Her heart quailed at the sight of the savagery unfolding around her. On the deck of the cog, a man had just driven his dirk through another's throat. As she looked on, aghast, he pushed his opponent overboard.

And then Astrid recognized the man who'd just killed his opponent.

It was Loch.

Clad in chainmail and leather, his long dark hair tied back with a thong at his nape, her brother whipped around to face his next attacker.

Astrid's lips parted as she watched him fight, her breathing stilling.

Aye, she'd seen her brother handle himself in the practice yard, but never in real combat.

Lord, he was vicious, and he wielded a dirk without mercy—stabbing and twisting, the long narrow blade glinting in the sunlight.

Moments later, the man he'd just engaged fell, howling, into the water.

Loch's gaze cut right then, toward her, and Astrid ducked her head. She didn't want him to spy her, for it would distract him. Distractions were deadly in battle.

Astrid clutched at the mast with her free hand as dizziness assailed her. Curse it, she needed to remember to breathe.

Her fingers gripped the bone hilt of her dirk so tightly, they started to ache.

More screams ripped through the late afternoon air, anguished and full of pain.

Astrid swallowed hard, even as bile stung the back of her throat. During the journey from Sanna, she'd tried to prepare herself for this, but there was no getting ready for the viciousness unfolding around her.

She was in the midst of hell.

25: SIDE BY SIDE

GLANCING AROUND, AS panic mounted in her breast, Astrid saw that the arrival of the Macleod birlinns hadn't gone unnoticed.

As they glided in, covering the last stretch of water to the cog, other ships that had been engaged in the fighting broke away, their oarsmen plowing through the foaming, bloody water to reach them. Feral cries split the air, and Astrid's bladder tingled.

The sound was animalistic.

This close, she could see the clan banners. The banner that fluttered from the bow of the nearest approaching galley wasn't Maclean but Mackinnon.

A heartbeat later, as the bow of their birlinn nudged the *Revenge Tide's* high clinkered sides, the Mackinnon boat intercepted them.

Steel flashed, and two huge men launched themselves across the foot of water separating the boats, landing with surprising lightness on their feet on the Macleod vessel.

Still clutching her dirk in a death grip, Astrid shrank back against the mast as a fast and violent skirmish ensued.

Malcolm and Finn were in the thick of it, fighting back-to-back, as they cut down their attackers. Splashes followed as men fell into the sea.

All the while, the birlinn rocked dangerously, water sloshing over the sides. Astrid's skirts were soon soaking.

She'd lost sight of her brother above.

God's blood, the *Revenge Tide* now crawled with men wearing Mackinnon sashes. She hoped that Loch had Logan Black fighting alongside him up there.

Her attention shifted then to where Finn now gripped the rigging with his left hand while he slashed at the next warrior to come at him with his right. His attacker wore a bright-red

MacGregor sash across his broad chest, his face a savage rictus as he ducked Finn's glinting blade and stabbed at him.

Finn handled himself well, yet the warrior had him right up against the edge of the birlinn. There was nowhere for Finn to go.

Astrid's gut clenched.

This would end badly; she had to help him.

Pushing her cloak aside, she resheathed her dirk. Her fingertips then slid across the worn knife belt at her hip. For years, she'd practiced knife-throwing in secret, her aim steadily improving to the point where she wished she could have competed with her father's men.

But she'd never been truly tested.

Meanwhile, the MacGregor warrior still slashed at Finn with single-minded brutality. A line of red had bloomed upon the side of Finn's lèine. If he hadn't continued clinging to the rigging, he'd have fallen into the churning water.

The sight of Finn's injury shocked Astrid into action. Rising to her feet and bracing herself against the mast with her left hand, she whipped the first of her knives out of her belt with her right.

And then, with a flick of her wrist, she sent the blade hurtling toward Finn's opponent.

It embedded with a meaty thud where the man's shaven head met the back of his nape.

Astrid's breathing stilled, her heart slamming painfully against her ribs as the MacGregor warrior froze. An instant later, the dirk in his fist clattered to the deck and his big body crumpled face down.

Finn pushed himself off the rigging, his gaze cutting from the twitching dead man at his feet to where Astrid clung to the mast.

Their gazes fused, and his hazel eyes glinted.

Bending over the fallen warrior, he yanked the throwing knife out of the man's neck and launched himself down the birlinn, reaching Astrid amidships as two more warriors leaped onboard.

"Astrid," he gasped, still out of breath from the fight. "Ye saved my life, lass ... I—"

"Later," she cut him off. "There's no time now."

He nodded, handing back the knife. "Here ... ye're going to need this."

Their fingers brushed as Astrid took the weapon, and the feel of his skin, warm and alive against hers, calmed the furious beating of her heart.

The moment between them shattered then, for two men, both bellowing, "Cuimhnich bàs Alpein,"—the Mackinnon war cry—clambered onto the birlinn, dirk-blades flashing.

"I'll take the one on the left," Finn grunted, turning to face them. "Ye kill his friend."

He didn't need to ask twice. Astrid's already blooded blade sank into the man's throat. Grasping at the embedded knife, his eyes wide and shocked, the warrior staggered back and disappeared overboard, taking Astrid's precious blade with him.

Fortunately, she had others.

Meanwhile, Finn ducked under his attacker's guard and shoved his dirk into his ribs, twisting hard, bringing him to his knees.

Panting, Astrid had just yanked the second knife from her belt when others still onboard their galley, Malcolm included, leaped from the railing. They climbed the rigging to reach the deck above.

Relief washed over her at the sight. Finally, her brother was getting the reinforcements he desperately needed.

Astrid expected Finn to go with them, yet he didn't. Instead, he moved back to her side, his gaze ensnaring hers once more. "We fight side by side, lass," he said, out of breath from the violent skirmish he'd just survived.

"Aye," Astrid gasped back, warmth spreading across her chest. "Side by side."

She was about to say something else when a large birlinn hove into view from behind the bulk of the cog.

Astrid caught sight of the Mackinnon banner flying from its mast, and her heart lodged in her throat. It was easily a forty-oar vessel with a red-and-white-checkered sail—one she'd seen before. A galley this size could carry a huge host of warriors.

She whispered an oath, her fingers tightening around the slender hilt of her throwing knife. Next to her, Finn ground out a curse of his own.

Kendric Mackinnon himself was bearing down upon them.

As the birlinn drew near, Astrid noted that it bore the scars of the days of battle it had endured. Chunks were missing out of the sides, and there were scorch marks all over its broad hull. There weren't as many warriors propelling it through the bloody water as she'd expected. As Astrid's gaze swept the deck, she counted no more than twenty.

Still, they were vastly outnumbered.

Yells rang down from above, and craning her neck, Astrid caught sight of men now descending the rigging toward them.

Her heart lurched.

Mother Mary, she hoped those warriors were Macleans or Macleods. If not, they were truly done for.

She caught a flash of auburn hair then and realized Malcolm was among them.

A moment later, the Mackinnon birlinn was alongside, and men lurched over the side. Some misjudged the distance between the two galleys and ended up in the water. Most of them bridged the gap easily though, catching hold of the rigging and hauling themselves aboard the Macleod birlinn.

What followed was a frenzied blur of violence that pushed any conscious thought from Astrid's mind.

All that mattered was that she and Finn now fought as a team—him with his dirk, and her with her throwing knives. Back-to-back amidships, they let their attackers come to them.

Knife after knife flew from Astrid's belt until it was empty. After that, she drew her dirk once more, moving forward with Finn protecting her to yank her throwing knives from those men she'd felled. Retrieving her precious blades, she slid them back into the belt at her hip with practiced ease.

Another Mackinnon lurched over the railing then, his gaze piercing hers. Astrid let her next blade fly. It caught him in the throat. Clutching at the hilt, he staggered backward and toppled into the churning sea.

Malcolm and a few of his men were with them now, yet they couldn't hold the tide back. It didn't matter how many men they brought down, more appeared.

Desperation clawed its way up Astrid's throat as she fought.

Aye, she'd dueled with the darkness and won, but she wasn't blind to their situation. The odds were against them.

And then, onboard the Mackinnon birlinn, she spied a big man with red hair threaded with silver. Her breathing caught as she recognized him. Dressed in chainmail and leather, Kendric Mackinnon cut an intimidating figure.

The last time Astrid had seen him, they'd been seated opposite each other in the great hall of Duart Castle. Loch had just promised the Mackinnon clan-chief her hand, and Kendric had worn a gloating expression as he swept his gaze over her in a proprietary fashion that made her hackles rise. Worse still, she'd seen lust spark in those cold silver eyes—a reaction that had terrified her.

But Mackinnon wasn't gloating or lustful now.

He was furious, his face twisted in savagery.

Feeling someone staring at him, the Mackinnon twisted then, his gaze seizing upon Astrid.

For a moment, his face slackened, as if he couldn't believe his eyes. However, he rallied quickly and rushed forward to the railing, bellowing at the men who now clambered aboard the Macleod birlinn, "Get the woman! I need her *alive!*"

A chill washed over Astrid at these words.

Aye, Kendric Mackinnon had wanted her. And now that he'd recovered from the shock of seeing the woman he'd planned to wed standing just a few yards from him, wielding throwing knives, a hungry look rippled over his face.

He thought he could capture her, could steal her away.

Astrid's belly hardened, rage quickening.

He wouldn't. She'd drive one of her knives through his heart first.

Curse it though, they were outnumbered. Malcolm and his men had moved amidships now, fighting with their backs to Finn and Astrid. Together, they were formidable, yet they were cut off, surrounded. Even though the likes of Malcolm Macleod fought with a skill and savagery that was breathtaking to behold, he couldn't stem the flow of Mackinnons who came at him.

Sweat and blood streaked their faces, exhaustion dragging at their limbs as they fought. Meanwhile, standing on the deck of his galley, Mackinnon watched, a cruel smile tugging at his lips.

He knew they were beaten.

Shouts rang through the air then—not cries of pain or anger, but jubilation. At first, Astrid thought the roar was coming from the Mackinnons as they closed in for the final push. Three of Malcolm's men had fallen, and those still alive slipped on the blood and gore that smeared the deck.

But no, the shouting wasn't coming from the Mackinnons, but from the men aboard the *Revenge Tide*. Some of them were pointing out to sea.

Her breathing coming in ragged bursts now, as she flung her last knife into the throat of a Mackinnon warrior who came at her, Astrid cut her attention east, beyond the bulk of the Mackinnon birlinn.

And for a heartbeat, Astrid just stared, unable to believe her eyes.

A large cog was sailing toward them, its emerald sail billowing, and a deep-red flag fluttering from its mast.

26: TOWARD THE LIGHT

A SOB CAUGHT in Astrid's throat. *"The Blood Reiver!"* she shouted, grasping at Finn's sleeve. "Look!"

Yanking his dirk out of the warrior who'd just tried to gut him, and shoving the man's corpse back so he slammed into the Mackinnon warrior trying to climb over the railing onto the ship, Finn did as bid.

He too stared for a moment before a grin split his face. "That canny bastard!"

Like Astrid, he hadn't believed Alec Rankin and his crew would ever come to their aid. Aye, Astrid had offered the pirate a considerable amount of coin, but he'd dismissed her offer.

He didn't involve himself in clan conflicts, he'd said.

And yet, here he was.

"Aye," Astrid gasped. "He must really want that kiss."

That comment earned a swift glare from Finn, although Astrid ignored his reaction. He couldn't have it both ways. Having made it clear that he didn't want her, he had no right to be jealous of other men.

Meanwhile, Kendric Mackinnon had also seen the pirate ship, its bloody flag snapping in the wind.

Bellowing orders, he turned from the Macleod birlinn to face the new threat.

Meanwhile, those aboard the *Revenge Tide*, clustered around the railing, to watch the approaching cog.

Relief weakened Astrid's knees when she spied her brother among them.

Loch's face was blood-splattered, and he was breathing hard, but he was alive.

Moments later, *The Blood Reiver* was upon the Mackinnon galley, and men, howling as they went, spilled over the sides of the cog, clambering down the rigging to meet the men defending their clan-chief.

The Macleods, Finn, and Astrid were all forgotten now.

The Mackinnon and his men were locked in a struggle for survival.

Glancing over her shoulder, Astrid looked, for the first time since being thrown into the midst of the battle, at Dounarwyse. Her breathing caught. The gates had been breached, and a melee was unfolding before them.

Astrid's heart started to hammer. God's teeth, the enemy was close to gaining entry to the broch. Was Jack, her cousin, amongst the men fighting before the walls, or had he already fallen?

Dread clutched at her chest at the thought. However, a roar from where Rankin's men had engaged the Mackinnons made Astrid jerk her attention back to the clan-chief's birlinn.

The pirates had broken through the ranks of men surrounding Kendric Mackinnon, and Alec Rankin himself, his blond hair tangling in the wind, battled the clan-chief. Both men fought with equal skill and savagery, although, right from the beginning, Rankin had the advantage, for he was younger, and the clan-chief was already tired after days of battle.

And as Astrid watched, hardly daring to breathe, Rankin pushed Mackinnon back toward the stern.

The clan-chief slipped then, losing his footing on the blood that now slicked the deck of his galley. An instant later, Rankin was on him, driving his dirk through the clan-chief's throat.

But the Mackinnon was strong, and even as he died, he grappled with his assailant, attempting to gouge Rankin's eyes out.

Eventually though, he choked on his blood, his big body twitching upon the deck of his birlinn.

Astrid gasped, a blend of horror and relief washing over her.

She couldn't believe it. The Butcher of Dùn Ara—the man who'd prevented peace from ever settling upon the Isle of Mull, was dead.

Slipping past Finn, she moved to the railing, her gaze sliding over the clan-chief's corpse. Around him, chaos reigned. With the Mackinnon dead, his men lost their focus.

Some tried to fight the pirates, desperation and despair twisting their faces, while others panicked and dove overboard.

Astrid let out a howl of victory, shaking her fist at them. The Mackinnons wouldn't prevail this time. Their clan-chief had fallen and now—

Something punched into her chest then, severing her jubilation.

Gasping, she staggered.

"Astrid!" Finn's voice sliced through the din of battle.

Time slowed as she looked down, cold washing over her when she spied a knife embedded to the hilt in the side of her chest. It had punctured her leather vest as if it were made of linen.

Where had that come from?

Pain hit her, flowering across her ribs. She fell backward, her arms wheeling as she tried to grab on to something. But her hands grasped nothing but air.

Finn was rushing toward her, his face stricken, his eyes wild, yet it was too late.

He was too far away.

Astrid hit the water with a slap, and it embraced her, pulling her under with breathtaking swiftness. The cold drove the breath from her lungs, and when Astrid opened her eyes, she was sinking.

It was quiet down here, below the churning surface of the sea, where bodies floated amongst a slick of dark blood. She could see the hulls of the four vessels that had been locked together in the final struggle.

The fighting was still going on, but in the deep, peace reigned. The water was turquoise, and schools of tiny fish swam by, oblivious to her plight.

Astrid's clothing, and the heavy cloak she wore, pulled her down.

Fight! Her mind screamed at her, railed at her. *Kick upward, toward the light.* However, she couldn't seem to move. The pain in her chest consumed her, and the strength had left her body.

The water was taking Astrid, and her vision narrowed, turning the watery underworld into a glimmering tunnel.

Yet, dimly, she was aware that something had pierced the surface of the sea high above her. A lean figure dove, his arms parting the water as he kicked down. The man's face was twisted with determination, his wide eyes looking around frantically.

Astrid's burning chest heaved. *Finn!* He was trying to save her.

She reached out, her numb fingers grasping.

His gaze seized upon her then, and he dove deeper still, his body arrowing toward Astrid. But the water slowed him down, pressing in at them both, thwarting him.

Astrid's vision dimmed now, weakness flooding over her. She could no longer fight it.

She sobbed, cold water rushing into her mouth, and a veil dropped over her sight.

A weighty silence settled outside the bedchamber.

"What the devil is the healer doing in there?" Jack demanded.

"Helping my sister," Loch replied wearily. "Donn's the best there is ... we just have to give him time."

Finn ground his teeth at these words and dragged his gaze from the closed door. He then glanced over at where the clan-chief stood a few feet away. Tension vibrated through Loch's muscular form. His face, smeared with blood and soot, was grimmer than Finn had ever seen it. Meanwhile, Jack fidgeted nearby; his expression was strained, his eyes hollowed.

They were all worried for Astrid.

She hadn't been in a good state when Finn carried her up here earlier.

After retrieving her from the water's chill embrace, he'd towed her to the pebbly shore. When she'd fallen in the water, he was transported back to another day—another lass. He hadn't been able to save Maggie, but he wouldn't let the sea take Astrid.

Fearing the worst as he lay her down on the beach, he'd been relieved to see she was, indeed, breathing, albeit shallowly. However, the sight of that knife protruding from her chest had quelled his jubilation. Knowing that it would be foolish to try and remove the blade, he'd carried her up to the castle, to where the battle had just ended. He'd been in pain as he climbed, the cut to his side stinging, but he just gritted his teeth and plowed on.

The slope beneath the broch was littered with bodies, the ground stained dark with blood.

But fortunately for both Finn and Astrid, the Macleans had emerged victors. Those Mackinnon, MacGregor, and MacNab warriors who'd survived the battle, and who hadn't fled for their lives, were now being rounded up.

Finn barely noticed the activity around him though. Instead, he'd picked his way over the fallen and stumbled into the barmkin, where he'd met Rae, the chieftain of Dounarwyse.

Rae's exhausted face had turned even more severe when he spied Astrid, insensible in Finn's arms. Without delay, he'd taken them straight into the tower house, to the healer. Luckily, Donn, the healer who hailed from Duart village, was already in residence. Loch had brought him with his force on the day they'd departed Duart, knowing that Donn's skills would be needed.

Finn had been relieved when the healer locked himself away with Astrid—with the Lady of Dounarwyse, Donalda, and Jack's wife, Tara, assisting him. But as an hour slid into two, and none of them reappeared, his thoughts took a bleak turn.

Such a lengthy wait boded ill.

"I was too slow," he spoke his fears aloud then. "I should have gotten to her sooner."

"Ye did all ye could," Jack replied roughly. Like Loch, he was filthy and still wore the chainmail and leather armor he'd been fighting in. Thanks to the assistance of the Macleods and the pirates, they'd managed to gain the advantage they needed on the water. And when the Mackinnon force on land got wind of their clan-chief's demise, their morale unraveled. It was said that the clan-chief's son, who'd led the attack on the castle, couldn't keep them together.

Outdoors, the folk of Dounarwyse were beginning the lengthy clean-up, tired yet thrilled voices filtering through the broch. But Finn couldn't feel the same joy, not while Astrid's life hung in the balance.

One of Loch's men arrived then, chain-mail clinking. "We've captured the last of the Mackinnons and their allies," he announced.

Loch favored the warrior with a brusque nod. "Good ... is the clan-chief's son among them?"

"Aye."

Something dark and violent moved in Loch's eyes. "Gather them outside the walls," he said after a pause. "I shall join ye shortly."

"Aye, Maclean."

Turning on his heel, the warrior departed.

Silence followed, and then Finn glanced over at Jack once more. His friend had started to pace the floor, his gaze shadowed.

"Satan's cods," Finn muttered. Jack's behavior was stretching his already frayed nerves taut. "Just calm yerself, man."

"I can't," Jack ground out. "I keep thinking about the Headless Horseman."

A chill washed over Finn at these words, yet Jack continued. "Ever since I saw the specter, I told myself that it likely had Loch, Rae ... or me ... in its sights. But what if it wasn't foretelling *our* deaths ... but Astrid's?"

"Stop it, Jack," Loch cut in, his peat-dark eyes, so like his sister's, guttering. "It's just superstition ... and has no power over ye unless ye believe it. Astrid is stronger than even she knows. She'll fight."

Finn's heart lurched. "Aye," he murmured. "She will." His mouth curved then into a brittle smile. "Ye should have seen her out there during the sea battle ... she was magnificent."

"Perhaps." A nerve flickered in Loch's cheek. "But she shouldn't have been there at all." He advanced on Finn then. "What were ye thinking, man, letting her fight?"

"Loch," Jack murmured, stepping forward and catching his cousin by the arm. "Let's not—"

However, Loch shook him off. Anger kindled in the clan-chief's eyes. "Ye threw my sister into the midst of carnage."

"I tried to insist that we drop her off farther south," Finn answered, holding his ground. "But ye know what Astrid is like. She refused. The only way I'd have gotten her back to Duart would have been by force."

"Well then, ye should have forced her."

Finn's fingers curled against his palms, his hands fisting. "I think not. Ye have already demonstrated what happens when ye try to *bully* Astrid into doing anything she doesn't want to."

Loch flinched at these words—yet he knew they were the truth. However, a moment later, his mouth pursed. "Don't try and twist this around to make it my fault."

"I'm just pointing out that yer sister has free will, and she exercised it."

Loch stared back at him, his gaze roaming over Finn's face now. A strange expression flickered over his features then, and he inclined his head.

"What?" Finn growled. He didn't appreciate the probing, assessing look the clan-chief was now giving him.

A few feet away, the door to the bedchamber opened and Tara Mackinnon stepped out. The woman, as lovely as she was, looked utterly drained. Blood splattered her steel-grey kirtle. Tara's flame-red hair had been tied back into a tight braid. Her eyes were red-rimmed, and her face was ghostly pale.

Finn's heart kicked hard at the sight of the blood, and at the grief he witnessed on her face.

Had they lost Astrid?

27: DEMANDING JUSTICE

"TARA?" JACK MOVED swiftly to his wife's side. "Are ye unwell?"

Tara shook her head, sagging against him. Her gaze swept to Loch and then Finn. "Donn has managed to extract the blade and staunch the wound ... Astrid still breathes."

It hit Finn then that the grief upon Tara's face wasn't only for Astrid—but also for her kin.

Earlier, Tara had been told her father was dead and her brother captured. Aye, she'd forsaken her family and wed a Maclean, but that didn't mean she'd cast her father—the brute that he was—from her heart.

Donalda appeared at that moment, wiping her bloodied hands on a cloth. Her heart-shaped face was tired, her small mouth pursed. "Astrid is sleeping now," she announced.

Loch moved forward, toward the chamber. Both women stepped aside to let him enter. Jack followed at his heels, with Finn bringing up the rear.

However, the sight of Astrid lying upon blood-stained sheets, her chest bound with a thick bandage, made Finn stop short.

Hades, she looked so vulnerable and frail. It was hard to believe this woman had fought at his side on the water earlier. Her skill with throwing knives was indeed impressive, and she'd found mark after mark with ease. Astrid had a warrior's soul trapped in a delicate body.

She'd saved his life. He'd wanted to thank her, but there hadn't been time. And now, he might never get the chance.

Finn's chest constricted then.

If she died, he'd never be able to look her in the eye and apologize for his behavior the night before. She'd never know that he was sorry. Guilt had weighed heavily upon him ever since their talk on the beach, for he'd seen the anguish ripple across her face before she fled to her tent.

He hadn't meant to hurt Astrid, yet her honesty had panicked him.

He couldn't let anyone in, least of all her. The lass he'd once pined for. The lady he'd once loathed.

Donn rose to his feet then, from where he'd been adjusting the bandage, and faced the clan-chief.

"Will she live?" Loch asked, the slight quaver to his voice betraying him.

The healer stared back at him, his sharp-featured face haggard. "I feared the blade might have pierced something vital ... but it did not," he replied, his gravelly voice carrying through the chamber. "However, yer sister has lost much blood, and there's a risk her wound might sour." He sighed then, reaching for a cloth to clean his hands. They were large and rawboned, farmer's hands, and yet they tended the sick and injured with infinite care. "All any of us can do now is wait."

Finn's breathing grew shallow at these words. He'd never been a patient man, yet there were some things he couldn't hurry.

Loch nodded, even if his face was still pinched with worry. "Stay with her, Donn," he said gruffly. "I have the Mackinnon prisoners to see to, but I will return as soon as I can."

A few feet away, Tara stiffened at these words. "Is my brother with them?"

Tara and Loch's gazes met and held for a few moments before he nodded.

A nerve flickered in Tara's pale cheek. "Then I'm coming with ye," she replied.

"Traitor." Bran Mackinnon's first words weren't directed at Loch, but the woman standing a few feet behind the Maclean clan-chief.

Observing brother and sister, Finn found himself silently impressed by Tara. Even exhausted and grieving, she held herself straight and proud, her chin high.

However, Bran's lip curled as he stared her down. The lad's fiery hair was tangled with mud and sweat, his fine hauberk was blood-splattered, and a deep cut marred his pale left cheek—yet he too stood tall, with that Mackinnon arrogance. Waiting at the front of the group of captives—a knot of bloody, injured men with bound wrists surrounded by pike-wielding warriors—he'd watched Loch's party approach with haughty defiance etched upon his face.

Quite a crowd had amassed before the walls. In the end, they'd all gone out to view the captives. Finn had followed Loch, picking his way through the chunks of debris that littered the barmkin and the bodies that were still being cleared away. The groans of the injured echoed against stone, while the aroma of stewing meat and baking bannock drifted out of the kitchens—a welcome scent after the rank odor of blood, sweat, and fear. However, once he'd left the barmkin behind, Finn smelled fear once more. Outside the broch, just a few yards away from the captives, the air was heavy with it.

The Mackinnon, MacGregor, and MacNab warriors bunched together, their faces pale and sweaty, as they awaited Loch's punishment. But their leader didn't appear concerned by the Maclean clan-chief's glare. Bran was too focused on his sister.

Tension pulsed between the siblings, yet Tara's gaze didn't waver. "We all made our choices, brother," she murmured.

A nerve jumped in his uninjured cheek. "Aye, and yers was to run off and shackle yerself to the enemy."

"Father didn't have my best interests at heart," she replied, even as her voice trembled. "So, I took my future into my own hands. Hate me for it, if ye will ... but I refused to martyr myself to appease our father."

"Heartless bitch!" His silver eyes glinted now, his hands, bound in front of him, clenching into fists. "Our father is dead. Slain by a Maclean!"

"Not a *Maclean* actually," an arrogant voice drawled, interrupting their exchange. "*I* killed him."

All gazes swiveled to the tall blond man standing behind Loch's party with the rest of the crowd, Malcolm Macleod and the three Maclean chieftains among them.

"The name's Alec Rankin ... Captain of *The Blood Reiver*," he continued, his gaze fusing with Bran's. His mouth then curved into a goading smile. "Ye should have yer facts straight, should ye ever need to go hunting for revenge."

In reply, Bran's face screwed up, and he spat on the ground. "*Pirate*," he snarled. "How much did they promise ye?"

"Enough."

A muscle worked in Bran's jaw, a sign that he was only barely keeping his temper leashed. Anger wouldn't help the lad right now though. Not while Loch was watching him with a narrowed gaze.

"Yer father managed to amass quite an army," the clan-chief spoke up then, drawing Bran's attention. "How is it that the MacGregors and the MacNabs assisted him so readily?"

Bran's mouth thinned as if he was considering refusing to answer Loch. Yet after a few moments, he grudgingly answered. "The MacNabs owed my father a blood debt from years ago ... and in exchange for eight galleys and a host of warriors, he promised the MacGregor clan-chief a marriage between his eldest daughter ... and me." Bran's silver eyes darkened then, hinting that he hadn't been pleased about the arrangement.

Loch nodded, taking this in. "My people would have me make an example of ye, Mackinnon," he said, his tone sharpening. "They'd have ye hanged, drawn, and quartered."

Tara's horrified gasp echoed into the afternoon air. "No!"

Loch ignored her, his gaze never wavering. "And as I look upon the devastation yer people have wrought, I'm inclined to agree with them."

Indeed, Dounarwyse's mighty curtain wall was pitted and scored, and the village beyond its walls razed to the ground. The fields had been trampled and spoiled too. It would take a long while for Rae Maclean to repair his broch and lands, and the past days had seen a great loss of life. The Macleans and their allies had emerged as the victors, yet this conflict had robbed them of much.

Bran's throat bobbed then, although the lad held on to his courage. Finn watched him closely, waiting for him to crack, for him to say he'd only been following his father's orders—for him to plead for his sorry life.

But he didn't.

Loch moved forward so that he and Bran only stood a couple of feet apart. "With ye dead, yer family line would be broken. Dùn Ara would be mine."

Bran visibly blanched at this. However, he still held his tongue.

"It would be only fair, wouldn't it?" Loch continued, his voice dropping to a threatening rumble then. "After all, yer father wanted to take my lands for his own. After Dounarwyse, Duart would have been his next target."

Bran swallowed once more, confirming his words.

Silence fell before the walls of Dounarwyse, and Finn marked the despair on the faces of the Mackinnon warriors. Tara was weeping silently now, and Jack had stepped close to her, wrapping an arm around her shoulders. Jack's face had shuttered though, giving no hint of how he felt about the clan-chief's threats.

Tension rippled through the warm air, and Finn's pulse quickened. Even though he wasn't a Maclean, he shared the outrage of those gathered beneath the broch. He too wanted to lash out.

The faces of those in the crowd looking on were taut, as if they hungered for blood. Meanwhile, Malcolm Macleod watched the proceedings with a glint in his grey eyes, while the three Maclean chieftains glowered at the captives. Leod Maclean of Moy, a big, swarthy man, wore a pitiless expression upon his angular face. Next to him, Logan Black, the new chieftain of Croggan, watched the captives with a narrowed gaze.

Of course, Black's family had been killed by Mackinnon warriors. He'd sought reckoning for a while now and had finally found it. Almost—for the clan-chief's son still breathed.

"I've seen enough blood over the past years to last me a lifetime, *lad*," Loch said, breaking the shivering silence. His eyes hardened now, his voice rough with menace. "Enough to sicken me ... but my clansmen demand justice, and I shall give it to them."

28: DO WHAT YE MUST

BRAN'S LIPS PARTED, a gasp wheezing from him. He staggered slightly then but managed to keep his feet. Next to him, one of his men rasped a prayer. "Do what ye must, Maclean," Bran finally replied roughly, even as the blood drained from his face. "My father would have shown ye no mercy ... so I expect none in return."

"No, please!" Tara wrenched herself away from Jack and rushed forward. And then, to everyone's surprise and shock, she dropped to her knees before Loch, craning her neck to stare up at him.

Tears streamed down her face, and despite that, like everyone else, outrage still beat in Finn's chest, the sight of Tara's desperation wrenched at him. "Spare their lives ... I beg ye!"

"Tara." Jack moved close then, reaching for her. "Come, love. Ye mustn't—"

However, she batted his hand away and grasped at Loch's legs instead. "The might of the Mackinnons of Dùn Ara is no more," she said, her voice shaking. "Aye, my father gathered an army and tried to crush ye ... but yer allies rallied, and yer victory is a great one. Ye have shown all of those who dwell upon the Western Isles the power and influence that the Macleans wield. After this, no one will dare oppose ye."

Finn's skin prickled at these words. But Tara hadn't yet finished.

"Aye, ye could take Dùn Ara for yer own ... could banish my clan from this isle, yet I beg ye to show us some mercy. Make my brother swear fealty to ye, and then send him home. Surely, the greatest punishment of all is for the Mackinnons of Dùn Ara to bend the knee to the Macleans of Duart?"

Loch raised an eyebrow as he looked down at Tara's bereft face. Nonetheless, he didn't step back from her, or reach down and remove her grasping hands from his legs. "Ye think my clansmen would prefer that to taking this whelp's life?"

"Aye." Tara's throat worked as she struggled to keep going. "The knowledge that yer clan is now the dominant one upon this isle, and that the Mackinnon clan-chief now answers to *ye*, would please them."

A snort followed these words. Logan Black had pulled a face, folding his powerful arms across his chest. He, for one, didn't look impressed by such a solution.

Meanwhile, Loch's brow furrowed. "There are some things only blood can mend, Tara," he replied.

"Aye, this is the way in the Highlands," Malcolm Macleod spoke up then. He'd watched the unfolding scene with interest, although he now wore a surprisingly sympathetic look as he viewed Tara. "We deal with our enemies harshly. How would Loch know yer brother would keep his word anyway?"

Malcolm's words caused a murmur of agreement to ripple through the crowd.

Swallowing, Tara kept her attention upon Loch. "Please," she whispered.

Finn could see she had nothing else to say, and it pained him to see a proud woman beaten. She'd done her best, yet she had no other argument to put forward. Her shoulders began to shake as she tried to keep her grief leashed.

"Loch," Jack said quietly. "I know it would break with the way of things ... but would ye grant Tara this? For her ... for *me*?"

Loch's gaze sharpened as it speared his cousin. "So, ye seek to manipulate me, do ye?" His mouth pursed. "Time was, ye'd be baying like a hound on the scent for me to sentence this lot to death." He jerked a thumb at where Bran and his men stood, silent and pale. "But yer choice of woman has skewed yer thinking."

"Aye, it has," Jack replied without hesitation, his attention never wavering. "Love has a way of blurring boundaries, as ye well know, cousin. Bran Mackinnon followed his father, aye, but should he be punished so severely for his loyalty? Do ye need to crush them to gain justice?"

Loch's frown slid into a scowl.

"Jack and Tara both have a point." To his surprise, Finn found himself speaking up then. "There are other ways to get even."

Loch's peat-brown eyes widened, while around them, a few of the men muttered under their breaths. Finn ignored them. He'd never been afraid to speak his mind or to risk unpopularity, although he couldn't understand why he felt the need to put his neck on the line now.

"Face it, Loch ... ye have never coveted Dùn Ara. Better to have the Mackinnon clan-chief kneel to ye." He jerked his head toward where Bran Mackinnon looked on, his face drawn, his silver eyes blazing. "Why don't ye get him to do it now?"

A bloody dusk settled over Dounarwyse, a crimson blaze that arched over the sky—a reminder of the violence that had unfolded here over the past days.

Finn watched it from the ramparts. After the meeting with the Mackinnon prisoners concluded, he'd retreated up here, leaving the others to retire indoors. Supper had come and gone, yet Finn hadn't gone in search of food or drink.

He had no appetite this evening. He only wished for solitude.

He couldn't stop thinking about Astrid, lying insensible in that sick room. She was under Donn's care, yet he wished there was something he could do to help her. Watching the sun slide behind the sharp edge of Dùn da Ghaoithe to the west, the largest mountain on this side of the isle, calmed his fears a little.

He was still watching the heavens when the scrape of a boot against stone roused him. Lowering his gaze and turning, Finn's attention settled upon where Loch strode toward him along the wall.

Unlike Finn, who still wore his blood and salt-encrusted leathers, Loch had bathed and changed into clean clothing. In one hand, he carried a skin of drink. However, his expression was inscrutable.

Finn tensed as Loch approached. He still couldn't believe his friend had heeded him, Jack, and Tara in the end. Under the eyes of all, he'd turned to Bran Mackinnon and given him a choice. Kneel before him and swear fealty to the Macleans, or he and the other prisoners would face execution at dusk.

It hadn't been an easy decision for the lad. Bran's gaze had glittered, his lean frame trembling with outrage and fear. Aye, he was proud, but he wasn't a fool. And so, as everyone looked on, he'd eventually lowered himself before Loch and sworn an oath to him, pledging loyalty to the Macleans for the rest of his days.

The words had cost him, each one almost sticking in his throat. It was humiliating indeed, and even though the other captives had been relieved that their lives were spared, Finn hadn't missed the scorn in their eyes as they looked upon the young man who now led them.

Finn wondered if Loch was angry about his interference and had sought him out to remonstrate with him. He was too bone-weary to argue, yet he readied himself all the same.

"Thought I'd find ye up here," Loch greeted Finn before thrusting the skin at him. "Here ... ye look like a man in need of some mead."

Finn gave a snort as he unstoppered the skin. He then raised it to his lips and took a deep draft. His throat was dry, and the sweet mead quenched his thirst. He then nodded his thanks.

"Bran Mackinnon will keep his word, ye think?" Loch asked, leaning against the wall and folding his arms across his chest.

"Aye," Finn replied. "Ye did right to let him and his men go."

Indeed, the new clan-chief of the Mackinnons and his warriors were currently traveling north, making for Tobermory on foot.

Loch raised a dark eyebrow. "Did I? Leod stormed off in a rage following my decision, and Logan Black looked as if he'd just swallowed a bag of nails."

"They'll recover."

Loch pulled a face. "I can't believe ye and Jack took Tara's side rather than mine."

There was a part of Finn that couldn't believe it either. However, the pain in the woman's voice, the grief in her silver eyes, had been unbearable to witness. "I suppose I'm getting soft-hearted in my old age."

Loch barked a laugh at this, the sound carrying down the wall and causing two warriors on the Watch to turn and look their way. Loch ignored them. Instead, his gaze settled upon Finn's face. "Soft-hearted ... ye?"

Finn's mouth compressed. He wasn't in the mood to be teased.

Heedless of his irritation, Loch flashed him a rueful grin. "I do believe my sister has done something to ye."

Hot and then cold washed over Finn, and he cut his gaze away, to stare at the fading sunset once more. "I don't know what ye mean," he replied, his tone cooling.

Loch snorted. "Let's not play games."

Finn's skin prickled, and still, he avoided his friend's eye. Tensing, he then braced himself to be heckled, mocked—but no such words were forthcoming. And when he glanced Loch's way once more, he found him viewing him thoughtfully.

"What?" Finn growled.

"There is definitely a change in ye."

"Ye are imagining things."

"I don't think so."

Clenching his jaw, Finn cut Loch a warning look. "Careful."

The clan-chief's dark eyes glinted. "I'm sure Astrid is behind it."

Finn sucked in a sharp breath. For a moment, he considered lying, but there was something in his friend's gaze that stopped him. It was a look that demanded honestly.

"It was that shipwreck," he eventually admitted. "When we were stranded together, we finally spoke of the past ... of Maggie's death. And I told her what I said to yer Da, about what really happened."

A beat of silence followed before Loch asked, "And what *did* happen? Ye never spoke of what passed between the two of ye in his solar."

Finn swallowed. He didn't want to admit such personal things to Loch. However, he could tell he wasn't going to let this be. And so, steeling himself, he replied. "Ye'll find this unbelievable ... but it was Astrid I wanted back then, not her friend. However, Maggie was sweet on me, and in the beginning, I encouraged her, thinking it might make Astrid jealous."

His mouth twisted as the memories flooded back once more. "It didn't … and Maggie grew more insistent. She was a fragile lass with an unhappy life at home, and she fixed her will upon me, determined that I should wed her. I will spare ye the details, but that day on the water, things turned ill between us when I refused to play her game, and she flew into a rage. She swam out to sea, and I followed her … but a rogue current pulled her under, and although I searched for her, she was lost."

Silence followed Finn's words, and the old guilt about Maggie tugged at him once more.

Loch's eyes shadowed at this news, and he gave a slow nod. "I imagined something of the kind had happened … although I had no idea ye pined for my sister."

Finn stepped back from the wall and raked a hand through his hair. "Aye, well, that's all done with now. She set the locals on me, remember?"

Loch grimaced. "Aye."

Silence fell between the two friends, and Finn heartily wished Loch would change the subject. Talking about Astrid made him feel light-headed and all twisted up inside. He took another deep draft of mead then, draining the skin. Stoppering it, he handed it back to Loch.

The bastard was still giving him one of his penetrating looks. "But *is* it done with?" he finally asked.

Finn frowned. "Aye."

Loch's mouth quirked. "Well then, ye won't be interested to hear that my sister is awake … and asking for ye."

29: THINGS UNSPOKEN

PROPPED UP ON a nest of cushions, Astrid sipped at the cup of bitter-tasting liquid that Donn held to her lips.

"I know it tastes vile, Lady Astrid," the healer said apologetically, "but it'll lessen the pain."

Astrid took a gulp and forced it down before favoring Donn with a wan smile. "Thank ye."

The healer smiled down at her, his eyes crinkling at the corners.

Their gazes held, and then Astrid heaved a sigh. "Ye must tire of me being so much trouble, Donn ... especially after I had ye so worried only six months ago?"

He shook his head. "That was different, lass. Then, ye carried wounds that were invisible to the eye ... whereas this time, I had to extract a blade from yer chest."

Astrid nodded, her gaze lowering to where a heavy bandage wrapped around her ribs under the loose night-rail she wore. "Will it sour?" she asked, a trifle tremulously. She'd seen several wounds, less serious than her own, turn nasty and take a life.

"It's too early to tell," Donn replied, "although I have packed it with woundwort, and I will stay by yer side in the coming days to keep an eye on it."

"I appreciate yer care," Astrid said, her throat thickening. Curse it, ever since she'd awoken, emotion would surge through her unexpectedly. She'd wept when Loch had come to see her, and when Jack and Tara had seated themselves at her bedside. Her cousin's eyes had gleamed with tears as he'd taken her hand and squeezed tight. "Ye did well, Astrid," Jack had said huskily. "I always knew ye were a warrior."

Astrid had appreciated his words, squeezing his hand hard in return as tears burned at her eyelids. Aye, she'd wanted to see them all, although there was one person who hadn't visited her yet.

Someone who was in the forefront of her thoughts. She'd asked Loch to fetch Finn, but he still hadn't been to see her.

A knock sounded at the door then, and Donn flashed her a smile before moving to answer it. "Word will be circulating the broch that ye are awake … prepare to be pestered," he said, hesitating then. "Although if ye aren't feeling up to it, I can send whoever it is away?"

"No, I'm well enough," Astrid assured him. In truth, she was as weak as a kitten. However, the draught he'd prepared her had dulled the throbbing ache in the side of her chest. "Come in," she called.

The door opened then, admitting a tall, lean figure clad in fighting leathers. Unlike her other visitors, Finn hadn't bathed and changed clothing. His face was haggard with fatigue, but his hazel eyes were as sharp as usual.

Before him, he held a tray of food. Astrid noted that he carried himself gingerly, and then she remembered he'd been cut during the battle.

"Pottage and fresh oaten bread from the kitchens, my lady," he greeted her, his mouth lifting at the corners. "If ye are hungry?"

Astrid nodded as she smiled back. Despite everything, she *was* hungry.

Donn gestured for Finn to approach the bed and set the tray down across Astrid's lap, which he did.

"I shall leave ye for a short while, Lady Astrid," he said. "I'm sure Captain MacDonald will look after ye while I get some supper of my own."

"I will," Finn assured the healer with a nod.

Astrid's heart fluttered as Donn made for the door. A moment later, it thudded shut and they were alone. Reaching down, she picked up the loaf of bread, tore off a chunk, and dipped it in the pottage. She then popped it into her mouth and chewed hungrily. "Ye can sit down, Finn," she mumbled, wishing her pulse would settle. "I hope ye've had that wound to yer flank seen to?"

He nodded. "It's just a scratch." He then pulled up a stool beside her. "How are *ye* feeling?"

"Like I've been trampled by a herd of sheep." She grimaced then. "Donn says it was a miracle that the blade didn't pierce anything vital."

Finn's throat bobbed. "Aye." He then cleared his throat. "I'm sorry, Astrid ... I should have been watching over ye more closely. That knife should never have found its mark."

Astrid shook her head. "Ye did all ye could." She swallowed another mouthful of bread, her gaze fusing with his. "*And* ye saved my life." Then, summoning her courage, she lowered the bread to the tray and reached out, boldly taking his hand in hers. "Thank ye."

Finn stared back at Astrid, his guts tied up in knots.

Seeing her like this—propped up in bed, her lovely face so pale, her dark eyes filled with gratitude—made him feel like a craven cur.

"It's *me* who should be thanking *ye*, lass," he said after a pause. "Ye saved my life too, remember?"

Her mouth curved. "Aye."

"I thought I might never get the chance to thank ye," he said, clearing his throat. "Or to apologize for what I said to ye on the beach at Sanna. I hurt ye."

Her eyes widened slightly at these words. A moment later, a blush bloomed across her cheeks. "It's all right," she murmured, glancing away. "Ye don't have to bring that up again."

Finn swallowed. Lord knew, he didn't want to either. Nonetheless, on the way up to her bedchamber, he'd told himself he would. "I just want ye to understand that ye did nothing wrong," he said, cursing the sudden huskiness in his voice. "The problem is entirely with me. Ye are lovely, Astrid. Kind and strong ... a fighter."

She glanced his way once more, watching him under long eyelashes. "My knife skills impressed ye then?"

He snorted. "Aye."

A pause followed, and he marked the way her gaze shadowed. "My bravery was all for show initially, ye know. I doubted myself, Finn ... it's why I insisted on fighting alongside ye all." Tension rippled across her face as she continued. "Ever since I went to pieces last year, I've feared there's a weakness inside me ... one that might consume me if I let it. I wanted to stamp it out."

Finn stiffened. "That's quite a test ye gave yerself, lass," he murmured. "One that could have killed ye."

Her throat bobbed, and she squeezed his hand. "I know ... but it clearly wasn't my time yet."

Finn's pulse quickened. He didn't want to remind her that she wasn't out of danger, that her wound might fester, and so he kept his fears to himself. Astrid needed those around her to keep strong, to believe she'd rally.

Unspeaking, he reached out and placed his free hand over hers.

The devil take him, he wished he was more eloquent. Astrid deserved better than his clumsy apologies.

Sweat dampened under his arms. *Speak to her, ye fazart ... explain yerself properly!*

But he didn't. He couldn't show his vulnerable underbelly—especially not to *her*.

And so, Finn ignored his heckling conscience and forced a brittle smile. "No, lass ... ye will be with us for a while yet."

Astrid's wound didn't fester. Instead, under Donn's care, it healed, and with the passing of the days, a bloom returned to her cheeks, and she grew stronger.

A week after the Siege of Dounarwyse, she was able to move about the broch without leaning on anyone for support. She was even well enough to attend the great feast Rae had put on to thank all the Macleans and their allies who'd helped defend his broch and remained afterward to assist the locals with starting the lengthy repairs.

Seating herself at the laird's table at one end of the hall—near where lumps of peat glowed in the large hearth, and Rae's two favorite highland collies gnawed at mutton bones—Astrid surveyed the cramped space.

Warriors—Macleods and pirates among them—sat shoulder to shoulder, calling out to the serving lasses who carried in spit-roasted suckling pigs, sides of venison, mutton pies, great wheels of cheese, and baskets of fresh bread.

The aroma was enticing indeed, and a smile tugged at Astrid's mouth.

It both surprised and pleased her that the Macleods and the crew of *The Blood Reiver* had lingered at Dounarwyse to help repair the damage the Mackinnons and their allies had wrought, but they had. And as she took a seat next to her brother at the laird's table, Malcolm Macleod caught Astrid's eye and flashed her a grin.

"It's good to see ye looking so well, Lady Astrid."

"Aye," Alec Rankin added from next to Malcolm. "Bonnier than ever."

Astrid smiled at them both in return, even as she caught Finn's glower. The laird's table was crammed this evening, and the Maclean allies had been given pride of place. Finn was seated a distance from her.

Catching his eye, Astrid inclined her head in a silent challenge. If he didn't appreciate the likes of Malcolm and Alec flirting with her, he could do something about it.

The problem is entirely with me.

She wasn't sure what he'd meant by that, and she'd waited for him to explain himself. Yet he hadn't. In the days that followed, neither of them brought up what happened between them at Dunvegan, or their fraught exchange on the beach at Sanna.

Whatever the reason, Finn had made it clear that their relationship could never go any deeper. And as frustrated as Astrid was by that, she had to accept his decision.

What a surreal week it had been. Dizzying relief had swept through her to learn that the Mackinnons and their allies had been bested. No longer would they live in fear that their northern neighbors would terrorize them. It was a great victory for the Macleans of Mull.

With the passing of the days, Astrid had received many visitors to her sickbed and had especially enjoyed lengthy chats with Tara. When they'd met at Duart a few months earlier, both women had been wary of each other. Yet now, a friendship had developed.

Astrid had also seen far more of Finn than she'd expected.

He was busy helping with repairs but still managed to find moments during the day to climb up to Astrid's chamber and look in on her. He'd stay with her a while then, and they'd chat about the goings-on in the keep. Sometimes, Finn would even tease her, revealing a dry, wicked sense of humor that often brought a grin to her face.

They'd even played a few games of knucklebones together, although the first time he'd drawn the bones from their pouch, Finn's gaze had guttered at the memory of the crew he'd lost. The pair of them had sat in silence then, their thoughts traveling to the brave warriors the sea had taken. They couldn't even give them a burial—something that would cause their kin additional anguish.

Shifting her attention back to where Malcolm was still eyeing her with a hungry look she didn't appreciate, Astrid swallowed a sigh. She wondered then if the warrior had stayed on at Dounarwyse to woo her.

Her pulse quickened at the thought. She hoped not.

Alec was also watching her with a hooded gaze, although his interest was far less evident than Malcolm's.

"I'm happy to see a blush upon yer cheeks," Mairi spoke up then. "It looks as if ye are truly on the mend."

Astrid smiled back at her sister-by-marriage. Loch's wife had traveled up from Duart for these celebrations and sat at her husband's side, her face glowing with relief and pride. "I am," she assured Mairi. "I'm happy to be able to move around again now ... I was getting so bored being confined to my bed."

"Aye, well, ye will be able to return to Duart tomorrow," Loch replied. "Does that please ye, sister?"

Astrid's smile widened, excitement fluttering up. Lord, she couldn't wait to spy the walls of her family's fortress rising against the sky, to greet the servants, and see her bedchamber again.

However, even through her joy, something inside her clenched.

She glanced Finn's way again to find him watching her with a veiled gaze. Would their return to Duart make things go back to the way they'd been before? Would the fragile friendship between them shatter when they were in familiar territory once more?

Enough, daft lass, she chided herself. *Worrying about such things won't help.*

Curse it, despite that she knew it was impossible, the longing in her breast couldn't be quelled.

She cared for Finn MacDonald. Deeply.

30: ASK ME TO DANCE

"THIS IS A victory that will be celebrated by the Macleans of Mull for generations to come." Loch's voice traveled through the hall. He then held his goblet of wine aloft. "The day we called upon our friends, and they answered."

The clan-chief's gaze traveled across the faces of those seated around him, lingering upon Captain Rankin and then Malcolm Macleod. Loch's cheeks were flushed with drink, and his eyes shone. "There are some things that will never be forgotten ... and if ye are ever in need, I will answer yer call without hesitation."

Silence fell. Staring back at Loch, Rankin's dark-blue eyes glinted, while next to him, Macleod's mouth curved into a smile.

Loch looked then to where Rae Maclean sat with his wife, Donalda, a few feet away. "Ye defended this fortress with the courage of a thousand men, Rae ... but of course, yer captain is a fierce warrior." He glanced over at Jack then, who'd slung his arm around Tara's shoulders. The cousins' gazes fused, a silent message passing between them.

Observing them, Astrid smiled. She was relieved to see that Loch and Jack had mended things. The situation with Tara had soured their relationship, and Loch had brooded over things afterward. But no longer, it seemed.

Her brother glanced *her* way then. "I thank ye too, sister," he said, his voice roughening. "Yer stout heart and tenacity brought the Macleods to our side when we needed them most ... and I'm relieved that ye are well enough to join us this eve." His attention flicked to Finn, and he lifted his goblet higher still. "And to ye, Finn ... ye stayed by Astrid's side and plucked her from the deep. I'm forever in yer debt, my friend."

Loch and Finn's gazes fused, the moment drawing out before Finn's lips curved into a smile and he nodded.

Clearing his throat, Loch then focused on the two men seated at the far end of the laird's table: Logan Black of Croggan and Clyde Maclean of Breachacha. "And without yer bravery, we would never have held Dounarwyse long enough for help to arrive," he said, his voice roughening slightly. "Ye fought like wolves, even when hope was fading."

Both Logan and Clyde nodded to their clan-chief, acknowledging his heartfelt thanks.

Warmth filtered through Astrid as she witnessed the emotion, the pride, that gleamed in the chieftains' eyes. Their loyalty to Loch was steadfast, and she was glad that Logan and Clyde had lingered after the victory, even if Leod Maclean stormed back to Moy Castle in a fury after Loch had spared Bran Mackinnon's life.

In truth, Astrid had been surprised to learn of her brother's choice, although when Finn told her what had happened—how Tara had begged for him to show Bran mercy, and how Jack and Finn had both spoken up—she understood.

Bran Mackinnon was no threat to the Macleans, and what better punishment than to have him kneel to those his clan had sought to crush? And kneel he had, in the dirt, at Loch's feet. He'd sworn fealty and even kissed the ring that Loch offered him.

A new chapter had begun upon Mull, one that would hopefully bring prosperity and peace.

There were a couple more speeches after that—as Rae stood up and spoke a few words, and then Malcolm Macleod had some things to say—before the feasting eventually ended, the trestle tables were folded up, and the benches pushed back against the walls.

Minstrels, perched upon the gallery at one end of the hall, struck up a series of melodies, some rousing, others gentle—and soon, dancers took to the floor.

Watching Loch hold Mairi in his arms as they danced together in the center of the hall, their gazes fused, Astrid's breathing constricted. The connection between her brother and his wife was a powerful one, and now Mairi carried his bairn. A few yards away, Jack and Tara also danced, and the love that shone on their faces was just as evident.

Both couples had weathered storms to find happiness, and yet here they were.

A wistful smile curved Astrid's lips. She then glanced across at where Finn sat, a cup of ale in hand. He wore a brooding expression now, although when he met her eye, his sharp-featured face tensed.

Astrid's smile faded. She held his stare, warmth pooling in her belly. *Ask me to dance.*

"Are ye well enough to dance, Lady Astrid?"

Shifting her gaze away from Finn, Astrid met Malcolm's eye. She was tempted to tell the arrogant clan-chief's son that she was too weak to take to the floor, yet that would have been a lie. And curse it, she wanted to dance. The minstrels were playing a lovely lilting melody that made her toes tap.

It wasn't Malcolm she'd hoped would approach her, but since Finn seemed glued to his seat, she wouldn't turn other men away. And so, she nodded. "Aye, Malcolm."

Flashing her a grin, he rose to his feet and held out his hand. Taking it, she let him lead her to the floor, where they were soon caught up in the dancing.

"Ye are lovelier than a misty spring dawn, Astrid," Malcolm said as he twirled her gently around him. "Don't think I haven't noticed ye."

Astrid's heart thudded at these words. Lord help her, he wasn't wasting any time. Not knowing how to respond, she kept a polite smile fixed in place.

However, Malcolm didn't seem to need a response, for he pressed on. "I have lingered at Dounarwyse to be of help, aye ... but I also wanted to ensure that ye were well."

"That is kind of ye," she murmured.

"And to ask ye to become my wife."

Astrid stifled a gasp at the blunt proposal. Malcolm was staring intently into her eyes now, supreme confidence upon his face. It dawned upon her then that he was sure she'd agree.

Moments passed, and Astrid decided that since he'd been so forthright, she would respond in kind. There was little point in being subtle with a man like Malcolm Macleod. "It is a fine offer, indeed ... but I cannot accept," she replied. Malcolm's handsome face tensed, his smoke-grey eyes narrowing, but Astrid continued, "I am sorry."

A brittle silence fell between them then. They continued dancing, yet Malcolm's mood had soured. He wasn't a man used to being spurned, even gently.

"I suspect I have a rival," he eventually muttered. "Can I ask who the whoreson is?"

Astrid frowned, her anger quickening. Her lips parted then, as she readied herself to answer, to tell him that was no business of his. "Ye have danced with the lovely Astrid long enough, Macleod." A tall man with a rippling mane of blond hair stepped up then, forestalling her response. "Allow the rest of us a few moments in her company." Alec Rankin flashed Astrid a rakish smile before inclining his head. "May I?"

Astrid swallowed a sigh. As attractive as Alec was, she didn't want to dance with him any more than she had with Malcolm.

The man she *did* want to take to the floor with still sat at the laird's table. She hadn't glanced Finn's way again, yet she felt the weight of his gaze, all the same.

Irritation pierced her then. *Let him stare.*

Meeting the pirate captain's sea-blue gaze, Astrid smiled. "Of course."

Malcolm muttered something ungracious yet stepped back. Perhaps he thought Alec had stolen her heart, for Astrid hadn't answered his rude question. And she wouldn't either.

The minstrels struck up another gentle tune—which Astrid was grateful for, as her injured chest was still bandaged and tender—and they began to dance once more. To her surprise, for a pirate, Alec moved with confidence and grace.

However, the way his gaze never left her face made misgiving flutter in her belly. *Dear God, not him too.* Fate seemed intent on mocking her this eve.

"Yer brother made good on yer word," he said after a spell, gently catching her by the waist and drawing her against him as the dance dictated. "My coin purse is now considerably heavier."

"Aye, well, ye and yer crew earned every penny," Astrid replied. "I didn't think ye'd come to our aid … but if ye hadn't, I'm not sure the battle would have turned in our favor as it did."

The pirate captain's sensual mouth curved. "Yer gratitude is appreciated, Lady Astrid … but do ye remember what else ye promised me?"

Astrid's breathing caught.

Curse it, she thought he'd forgotten about that. "The kiss, ye mean?" she replied, feigning a lightness she didn't feel.

"Aye."

Her heart started to race, warmth rising to her cheeks. "Surely, my thanks is payment enough?"

Alec's smile turned wicked. "Oh, but a passionate embrace would make it all the sweeter."

"Kiss her, Rankin, and I'll knock yer teeth down yer throat."

Astrid's gaze cut right to see that Finn was no longer seated at the laird's table, nursing an ale. Instead, he'd pushed his way through the dancers and was striding toward them, cutting a swathe through the crowd.

"Finn," Astrid greeted him, a warning in her voice. "There's no need to be heavy-handed, I was—"

"About to give this rogue a kiss!"

Astrid drew herself up, heat igniting under her ribs. "No, I wasn't."

"Ye weren't?" The disappointment in Alec's voice was evident, even if he wore a smirk now. "Ye still haven't managed to leash that hound of yers, Lady Astrid."

Anger surged, hot and dangerous, through her. "He's not my *hound*."

She was vaguely aware then that, around them, the music had died, and the dancing had stopped. Everyone, including her brother and her cousin and their wives, was staring at them.

Embarrassment flamed across her face, yet she straightened her spine.

A scene like this was the last thing she wanted, although she wasn't going to take the blame for Alec Rankin's brass neck or Finn's rudeness.

Cutting her attention back to Finn, she marked the anger on his face, the way his hazel eyes had gone a murderous green as he glared at the pirate. Alec's big body tensed in response, his brow furrowing.

Disappointment, tinged with a little disgust, swooped through Astrid, and she took a step back. She didn't understand him at all. What right did he have to be jealous? If the two of them wanted to pummel each other, let them. She wanted no part of it.

However, to her surprise, Finn's hand shot out and lightly caught her by the wrist, drawing her toward him.

His attention shifted to her face then, and his expression softened. "I owe ye yet another apology, lass," he said huskily. "I don't have Rankin's charm or Macleod's brash confidence … but I'm done hiding."

31: A THOUSAND-FOLD

FINN'S COMMENT BROUGHT a wave of whispers around them and raised another smirk from Alec.

Astrid ignored them all as she stared back at Finn. "Excuse me?"

"I haven't been honest with ye," he replied, his gaze never wavering. "Or myself."

Astrid swallowed. They were making a scene, and her cheeks were aflame, yet she couldn't look away from him. "Tell me the truth then," she whispered. "Now."

A flush rose to Finn's high cheekbones. "I was a coward all those years ago ... scared that ye'd reject me," he admitted, his voice rough now. "And it galls me that I'm still a fazart when it comes to matters of the heart."

Her mouth quirked, even as her throat thickened. "I would never have taken ye for a coward, Finn."

He gave a soft snort. "Aye, well ... now ye know the truth." He stepped in closer, blocking out the rest of the hall. "I'll admit I didn't have the best start to life, but it was me who carried things on. I made myself an island ... and decided I was better off that way." He swallowed then. "But I was wrong."

Astrid's breathing caught at this admission. She wasn't sure how to answer him, but it appeared Finn didn't require an answer.

"Ye are everything I've ever wanted and yet been terrified to reach for," he continued huskily. "Aye, there are better men out there ... but none would adore ye as fiercely as I do." He drew her closer still, his arm curving around her waist. The feel of his touch made her want to sink into him, even as her pulse went wild. "None would cherish yer independent spirit and unique blend of fire and softness ... as I do."

Astrid's lips parted. His admission had robbed her of words.

Nonetheless, Finn still wasn't done. "Ye own my heart, lass," he admitted, his gaze never leaving hers. "And although it terrifies me to ask ye this, I must. Are my feelings returned?"

"Aye," Astrid gasped without hesitation. "A thousand-fold."

A wide, delighted smile creased Finn's face at her response. It was like watching the sun come out after days of heavy fog.

He tore his gaze from hers then and focused on where Loch stood a few yards away, his arm slung around Mairi's shoulders. The clan-chief and his wife were watching them; Loch wore a knowing smile while Mairi looked bemused.

"I'm in love with yer sister," Finn informed him, his voice carrying over the now silent hall. "And with yer permission, I would make her my wife."

Murmurs followed this comment, even as Astrid's belly swooped as if she'd just leaped off a cliff. Mother Mary, had he just proposed?

All gazes swiveled to Loch to see how he'd react. Of course, it was an unconventional match. Astrid was a clan-chief's daughter while Finn was the Captain of the Duart Guard. By rights, she should have chosen a man of the same rank as a husband. Also, few of them would have forgotten that he'd once promised his sister to Kendric Mackinnon to forge an alliance between their clans—and perhaps they thought Loch had another husband in mind for her.

The clan-chief didn't answer for a few moments. Instead, his gaze moved from Finn's face to Astrid's. "Is this what ye want, sister?" he asked eventually.

"Aye," she replied firmly. "More than anything."

Her emphatic statement drew more murmurs, although many folk in the crowd, Jack and Tara among them, were now smiling. Meanwhile, Finn's hold on her waist tightened.

Tension shivered through his lean frame.

Loch gave a slow nod and focused once more on Finn. "Then ye have my blessing."

Joy sparkled in Finn's hazel eyes, and his throat worked as emotion swept over him. "I will protect her with my life," he said, voice catching. "I swear."

Loch moved close, covering the space between them and placing a hand on his friend's shoulder. "There's no need for ye to make such a promise, lad," he said gently. "I know I railed at ye when Astrid was injured ... but I was wrong to do so. Ye've already proved to me that ye'd do anything to keep my sister safe." He paused then, favoring them both with a wide smile. "And if ye wish it, I shall join ye as husband and wife here and now."

It was incredible how events could take a turn.

Earlier, Astrid had believed Finn would never let his defenses down around her. But in the space of a few moments, he'd declared his love for her before a packed hall and gained her brother's blessing for their union. And Loch had offered to marry them.

They both agreed.

Standing in the heart of the hall, as the clan-chief wound a length of Maclean plaid about their joined hands, Finn and Astrid stared into each other's eyes. The ceremony was short yet heartfelt, and as Astrid promised that she would be Finn's, body and soul, until she drew her last breath, a sense of completeness filtered over her.

This was how things were meant to be.

"As yer hands are bound together by this plaid, so, too, shall yer lives be bound." Loch's voice rose into the smoky air. "May ye forever be one, sharing in all things, in love and loyalty for all time to come. May the road rise to meet ye. May the wind be always at yer back." He then unwound the plaid and stepped back. "Ye are now husband and wife." His mouth quirked into a grin. "So, ye can stop gazing at my sister with calf eyes and kiss her, man."

A heartbeat later, Finn did just that, scooping Astrid gently against him, his mouth slanting across hers. And she kissed him back just as fiercely, as cheering erupted around them, shaking the rafters.

The rest of the evening passed in a blur.

More wine, mead, and ale were brought out, as were little honey cakes, which the cooks had hastily prepared upon hearing a wedding would take place that very eve. Fresh out of the oven and oozing with honey, the cakes were hot and delicious.

However, Astrid barely tasted them. All she could think about was that she and Finn were wedded. Seated next to each other at the laird's table, their thighs pressed close, she was exquisitely aware of him. Each moment became more tension-filled than the last.

And when Finn fed her some cake, she boldly licked the honey off his fingers.

The hunger that ignited in his eyes made her tremble, and their gazes fused, need shivering between them.

It had been a few days since their encounter at Dunvegan Castle, yet neither of them had forgotten it.

Long moments passed, and then, wordlessly, Finn rose from the table and drew Astrid to her feet as well. Without warning, he scooped her up into his arms.

Astrid squeaked, and Finn's gaze snapped to hers, shadowing. "Did I hurt ye?"

She shook her head before wrapping her arms around his neck. "No," she whispered. "Ye just took me by surprise."

A smile tugged at the corners of Finn's mouth, and need quickened in Astrid's stomach. When he looked at her like that, something deep inside her caught fire.

Ribald comments followed them as Finn carried his bride away from the laird's table, skirting the dancers, and making for the door. Neither of them paid the others any mind, even if Astrid marked the scowl on Malcolm's face and the smirk upon Alec's.

Finn didn't speak as he carried Astrid upstairs. There had been no time for servants to prepare them a bridal chamber, or for a priest to bless the bed, but Astrid didn't care.

All she wanted was to lie with this man, to let the love they'd just admitted and formalized flow.

Entering Astrid's bedchamber, Finn nudged the door closed with his foot and lowered her to the ground. And then, he dipped his head once more and kissed her. This embrace was slow and tender.

Tears stung Astrid's eyelids as the kiss drew out, their tongues stroking, his hands reverently cupping her face.

And when Finn eventually drew back, gazing down at her, Astrid's vision blurred, emotion swelling in a tide within her. "I love ye, Finn," she gasped out the words. "It's only ever been ye ... I just didn't want to admit it."

"My lovely lass." His voice caught as his thumb swept away the tears that now trickled down her cheeks. "What did I do to deserve ye?"

Astrid huffed a shaky laugh. "I'm just sorry we wasted so much time," she admitted huskily. "All these years loathing each other ... never realizing that we were meant to be together."

"Aye," he said, his voice thick now. "And I won't waste another moment." His mouth found hers again, and this time, it quickly slid from tender to passionate.

Astrid matched him, her arms winding around his neck, her body pressed against his long, lean length.

This eve, Finn wasn't dressed in his usual tight-fitting leathers. Instead, he'd donned a fresh lèine, tucked into chamois braies, a Maclean sash across his chest. The clothing softened him, suited him. Although there was nothing soft about his hard-muscled body, or the rod that pressed against her stomach as their kiss grew wilder and deeper.

No, his arousal was very much in evidence, and Astrid found herself grinding her hips against him, as she had that night in Dunvegan, desperate to feel his body against hers.

Breathing hard now, Finn drew back. "Are ye strong enough, Astrid?" he asked, his voice gravelly with need. "I don't want to hurt ye."

"I'm fine," she assured him, "as long as this isn't rough."

"I will never be rough with ye," he assured her, as he moved behind her and began unlacing her surcote. His tone grew huskier still then as he added. "Unless that is what ye wish."

Heat pulsed in Astrid's lower belly at the sensual promise in his voice.

How she wanted him, *yearned* for him.

Wordlessly, Finn undressed her, stripping off her surcote and kirtle, and the filmy lèine she wore underneath, until she stood before him, naked save for the light bandage that covered her ribs. The wound still had a large scab upon it, and Donn wished to keep it protected during the day.

Embarrassed, she adjusted the bandage slightly. "Apologies about this," she murmured. "It isn't the bonniest sight."

Finn's hungry gaze swept over her. "It makes no difference to yer loveliness, lass."

Astrid's breathing caught. Hades, the gleam in his eyes, the way his lips parted, made her heart thump against her ribs.

"Ye are bonnie enough to break my heart," he added.

"I never would," she whispered, even as heat washed over her.

Heart pounding now, she stepped close to him, her hands straying to where his lèine was tucked into his braies. "Come," she murmured. "I want to see ye naked too."

32: WAITING MY WHOLE LIFE

FINN'S MOUTH CURVED, even as his pulse took off.

Did this woman know just how much she inflamed him? Astrid was as slender as a willow reed, and the sight of her bandaged ribs made his chest tighten. He didn't want to hurt her, yet the way she was looking at him now—a challenge glinting in those peat-colored eyes—made something feral stir within him.

Their previous encounter had already given him a taste of her. But this time, he wouldn't back away. This time, he intended to lose himself inside her.

No more excuses. No more lies.

She was his, and he was hers.

Finn pulled off his lèine, noting the way Astrid's hungry gaze swept down over his nude torso to where he was now unlacing his braies. He removed those too, swiftly, eagerness thrumming through him.

Lust arrowed through his gut when Astrid gave a soft, breathy gasp, her lips parting as she stared at his rod.

Glancing down, he marked how swollen and hard it was, how it strained against his belly.

"Can I touch it?" she asked, her voice catching with excitement.

"Aye," he ground out.

"Show me how."

"Lower yerself to yer knees."

Lord, it felt sinful to give such a command, and he thought Astrid might hesitate. Yet she didn't. Instead, her chest heaved, her eyes shining now. An instant later, she sank down before him.

She reached out then, her fingertips tracing his length, from root to tip.

Finn sucked in a breath, his rod jerking under her touch. Jaw clenched, he took hold of her hands, showing her how to stroke his bollocks with one and fist his shaft with her other, working him slowly with just the right pressure.

"Oh, Jesu," Astrid murmured. "It's getting even bigger ... even harder."

Finn ground out an oath, even as his rod swelled further at these words. "It's yer touch, mo chridhe," he rasped. "Ye are driving me to the edge."

Astrid gazed up at him, a smile curving her rosebud lips. And then, to his surprise, she leaned in, her mouth capturing the slick tip of his rod as she tasted him.

Finn's curse echoed through the chamber. His hands went to her hair, tangling through its softness to hold her steady. He guided her then as she sucked him hungrily, her tongue exploring the swollen head of his shaft.

Astrid was an eager pupil, and a quick learner too, as she stroked, licked, and sucked him with a greed that stoked a heat in his gut.

She'd have continued, would have pleasured him until he spilled deep into her throat, if he hadn't stepped back and withdrawn from her.

Breathing hard, even as she made a frustrated sound and reached for him, Finn gently hooked his hands under her armpits, lifting Astrid to her feet. Then, he climbed onto the bed, drawing her with him, positioning her so that she was on her knees astride his lap. Meanwhile, he leaned his back against the mound of pillows at the head of the bed.

Astrid's high, peaked breasts were level with his face now, and he brushed his rough cheek against her swollen, sensitive nipples. Hunger spiked through him yet again when she gasped and arched her back, pressing her lovely paps into his face.

Finn caught one of her needy nipples with his mouth, suckling her gently, while she trembled and gasped in his arms.

Hades, she was so responsive—as she had been the last time he'd pleasured her. It made him ache for her even more.

Trying to ignore his throbbing, pulsing groin, he moved to her other breast, while he trailed his fingertips down over the arch of her ribcage and the hollow of her belly, to the damp pale-gold curls beneath.

And when his fingers slid into the slippery cleft between her thighs, Astrid cried out. She then moved her legs farther apart, giving him greater access, allowing him to stroke and tease her until her whole body was shuddering, her breathing coming in short, ragged gasps.

But Finn was relentless. He knew what she needed, and his fingers continued to play her like a lyre until wet heat surged against his fingers, until she gasped out his name as she held tight to his shoulders.

Angling his chin upward, he met her gaze then.

Until his dying day, he'd never forget how beautiful Astrid Maclean was at that moment. Her face flushed from her release, her lips bee-stung from his kisses, and her eyes gleaming with desire.

An ache rose in his chest.

This bonnie creature was *his*. He hardly dared believe it was true. "Are ye ready, love?" he asked.

Astrid nodded, catching her lower lip with her teeth as she reached down and wrapped her fingers around his throbbing shaft, angling it between her trembling thighs. "Please," she whispered.

Finn stifled a groan. Her touch nearly undid him, as did her husky plea. She didn't need to beg for this, yet the fact she did ignited a wildness inside him that made it difficult to go slowly.

But she was a maid, and he didn't want to hurt her.

As such, he took hold of her hips gently and guided her down upon him, inching into her a little at a time. After a few moments, he stopped, to let her adjust to him, before continuing the slow, sensual slide.

Astrid groaned, circling her hips upon him.

Finn hissed through his teeth. Christ's blood, how could he go slowly when she moved like that? The feel of her tight, wet quim enveloping him was so good, he was starting to lose his wits. "Astrid," he choked out. "Don't—"

She didn't heed him though. Instead, with a sharp cry, she sank down on him hard, bringing him deep inside her. And then, even as his hips bucked up to meet hers, she ground herself onto him.

Finn cursed, gripping her hips tightly as he urged her to repeat the action.

Hades, this was supposed to be slow and gentle. However, with Astrid writhing on his rod like a temptress, he lost all coherent thought.

She wore a fierce, hungry look upon her face now, as if she too had forgotten that they were supposed to be careful. And when Finn arched up and rolled his hips against her, Astrid's breathing caught in a sob of pleasure.

"Do ye like that, lass?" he growled, repeating the act.

"Aye!" she cried, her gaze seizing with his. "Don't stop, *please* ... oh!"

Gripping her hips tight, he slid her up and down his rod. God help him, she was gloriously wet now, her quim clutching at him with each delicious stroke. It was so good that Finn's eyelids fluttered. The urge to throw back his head and let himself go rose inside him then.

However, he didn't want to break eye contact with Astrid. Somehow, staring into her eyes as he took her made the pleasure even more intense.

Watching the flush that flowered across her face, seeing how her lips parted to gasp as he pulled her closer against him, and how her eyes grew wide, excited him just as much as the feel of being buried inside her.

Finn had swived his fair share of women over the years, yet he'd never experienced anything as intimate as this, had never fully let himself go.

But he did now. His body trembled as pleasure churned in his belly, heat gathered in his lower back, and his bollocks drew painfully tight.

It had never been this good. Never.

Astrid shrieked then, her lissome body writhing against him, her sweat-slicked skin gleaming in the lantern light as she shuddered her release.

And all the while, her core clutched at him, milked him. It was too much.

A shout tore from Finn's throat, and he bucked up, slamming home one last time, deep inside her.

Cradled in Finn's arms, their ragged breathing the only sound in the bedchamber, Astrid buried her face in the hollow of his neck, breathing in his scent, reveling in the delicious feel of him still buried to the hilt within her.

Lord, that was incredible, better than any heated fantasies that her mind had led her on after their encounter in Dunvegan Castle.

The intensity of it—the way their gazes had held the entire time, and the way that his shaft felt as if it were piercing her soul with each thrust—had completely undone her.

In the aftermath, her limbs were liquid, and her pulse still throbbed through her womb.

To think that they could do that, again and again, for they were now wed, made her breathing quicken and heat flicker to life once more in her lower belly.

She could hardly wait.

Eventually, sufficiently recovered, Astrid raised her chin, her gaze lifting to his.

Her breathing caught. Finn's hazel eyes shone; his face was more vulnerable than she'd ever seen it.

They stared at each other, the intimacy and truth of the moment vibrating between them, and then Finn reached up, brushing aside the hair that had stuck to her sweaty cheek.

"I've been waiting my whole life for that," he admitted huskily.

"Me too," she whispered.

"It's as if something has just unfurled inside my chest," he continued, his voice catching. "As if a knot I've carried all my life has suddenly released." His eyes glistened then, a tear escaping and rolling down his cheek. Finn's chest hitched, and he lifted a hand to dash the tear away. "Satan's cods, what's wrong with me ... I haven't wept since I was a wee bairn."

Astrid's mouth curved, even as tenderness rose within her. "Don't brush yer tears away, love ... there's no shame in them." Her throat thickened then, and she cupped his cheek before lowering her lips to his for a tender kiss.

"I'm not used to feeling this ... vulnerable," Finn admitted then, his breath mingling with hers. "I've never truly let anyone but ye in. Ye alone understand me, lass. When I'm with ye, I know I've come home."

33: DRAGONS TO SLAY

A GOLDEN DAWN rose over the sea, greeting Astrid and Finn as they climbed up to the walls together.

Astrid had donned a light woolen cloak, for the air was unseasonably cool for May.

It was early, and the guards on the Watch cast the couple a surprised glance.

"Didn't expect to see ye up so early after yer wedding night, MacDonald," one of them ribbed Finn.

"Aye, well, I'm not one to lie abed," he replied without breaking his stride, his tone dry.

The guard huffed a laugh, while Astrid's cheeks warmed.

Of course, after the spectacle they'd put on for everyone the night before, they'd be the talk of the broch. She'd been so caught up with joy, so enthralled in Finn, that she hadn't noticed or cared how the others reacted.

This morning, however, shyness overcame her.

She'd always been private when it came to personal matters, as had Finn. They'd yet to join Rae and Donalda to break their fast in the chieftain's solar, and she'd have to brace herself for some good-natured teasing from Loch and Jack, and likely hugs from Mairi and Tara. Not that she didn't appreciate them all being happy for her and Finn—only that she squirmed at being focused on so intently.

"Ye'll get used to it, mo chridhe," Finn murmured when they were out of earshot of the guard. "Folk will tire of us after a while." He paused then, flashing her a warm look, his mouth quirking. "And it's good for them to focus on something joyful … after so much bloodshed."

Astrid nodded, her mood sobering as she recalled the fresh graves she'd visited the day before—her first trip out of the broch since the battle—in the kirkyard on the fringes of Dounarwyse village.

There had been so many of them. So many warriors who'd never return home to their wives and bairns. So many hearts broken.

"I've never felt such conflicting emotions," she admitted then. They'd stopped at the farthest edge of the eastern walls and were now gazing across the sea at where the rising sun had turned the water into molten gold. "How is it possible to be so happy, and yet grieve at the same time?"

"Ye've always had a big heart, lass," Finn replied, putting an arm around her shoulders, and allowing Astrid to lean into him. "It's one of the many things I love about ye."

Astrid tilted her chin to meet his eye, favoring him with a soft smile. "It's a relief," she murmured then, "not to fear my own nature any longer. After everything we've been through of late … and the battle … I feel as if I've slayed a dragon."

Finn's mouth quirked. "We all have our dragons to slay." He lifted his hand then, brushing her cheek with his knuckles. "But ye mustn't condemn yerself for despairing last year. Loch did wrong trying to force ye to wed a man against yer will … he nearly broke yer spirit, and he'll always regret it." Finn's expression tightened then. "And I showed ye no pity either at the time … and for that, I'm sorry."

"We were enemies then," she pointed out with a rueful smile. "I would have thrown yer compassion back in yer face."

Finn laughed. "Aye, ye would have … blade-tongued shrew that ye were."

Astrid snorted, digging a playful elbow into his ribs. "Watch yerself, MacDonald."

Still laughing, he drew her close, and, together, they turned and looked out to sea. A companionable silence settled between them. It relaxed Astrid to find that they were both content to be in each other's company without speaking.

However, Astrid spotted something then—a rowboat angling through the gleaming water, heading toward the jetty that thrust out into the water below the broch. "It looks like Dounarwyse has visitors," she murmured, peering at the figures in the boat. "Two of them."

"Aye," Finn murmured, his gaze tracking the rowboat as it approached the jetty.

Presently, the craft reached its destination and one of the figures jumped out and tied the boat to the mooring.

Even from here, Astrid could make out a man and a woman. He was broad-shouldered and powerfully built with a shock of ginger hair, and she was small with long braided dark hair. A wee dog, a terrier, leaped out of the rowboat then, yipping with delight as it capered along the jetty.

A flicker of recognition tickled at Astrid as she peered at the couple. She didn't recognize the woman or the terrier, yet the man seemed familiar.

A moment later, she gasped. "God's blood, Finn ... it's Dougie!"

Her husband stiffened against her. "What?" He moved forward, to get a closer look. "Are ye sure?"

"Aye!"

Joy surged through Astrid, beating like the wings of a freed bird. She'd believed all the crew of the *Sea Eagle* had lost their lives, but at least one hadn't. Somehow, Dougie, the youngest of her escort, had made it to shore.

And now, he'd reached Dounarwyse.

The couple was walking, hand-in-hand, up the slope toward the castle gates.

Finn murmured an oath then. "That's Dougie all right." He cut her a look, his eyes shining. "I don't believe it."

Their gazes fused, and then they both turned from the wall and headed toward the stairs that led back down to the barmkin. "Come, love." Finn caught Astrid's hand as they descended to the barmkin. "Let's give the lad a rousing welcome."

EPILOGUE: WHAT OUR LOVE HAS MADE

A year later ...

"MOTHER MARY, I'm getting as fat as a Yuletide goose!"

"Never!"

"It's true." Astrid struggled out of her chair, leaning back to keep her balance. "My belly arrives in every chamber I enter three strides ahead of me."

Mairi snorted a laugh, even as she bounced her bairn, Greig, upon her knee. "Nonsense."

"I'm afraid it isn't." Astrid ran a hand over her swollen midsection. "I've even started waddling!"

"I did too," Mairi replied with a rueful shake of her head. "Greig was a big lad." She chucked the bairn under the chin, and he giggled. "Weren't ye?"

Astrid grimaced, nervousness fluttering up. Greig's birth had been a long one, and Mairi's shouts and cries had echoed through the hallways of Duart Castle for many hours before the lad had come bawling into the world.

Astrid hoped the birth of her bairn, which the midwife said was just days away now, wouldn't be as long or as painful.

She wasn't the only one of their family with bairn at present. Tara had recently shared the news that she was also expecting. However, she wasn't due until near Yuletide.

Moving to the window of the ladies' solar, Astrid's gaze traveled over the inner courtyard, where a servant was sweeping the cobbles with a large broom. It was a balmy afternoon, the air sweet with the smell of summer. As well as the rhythmic sound of the broom, the clang of iron from the weaponsmith's forge in the outer courtyard, and the rumble of men's voices, drifted into the solar.

A tall, lean figure clad in leather stalked into view then, upon the wall opposite—and despite that they'd been wed a year now, the sight of her husband made Astrid's breathing catch.

Feeling the weight of her stare, Finn slowed his step and turned toward her.

Their gazes fused, and his mouth quirked into a soft smile that he reserved only for her.

Astrid smiled back.

This past year had been such a happy one.

Life had changed considerably for both her and Finn upon their return to Duart Castle. For one, she'd decided to move out of the keep and into Finn's lodgings high up in the guard tower. It was more simply furnished than her old bedchamber, yet larger, and Astrid liked having her own private space. Recently, she'd taken on Dougie's wife, Garia, to help cook and clean. Garia, whose practical and sweet nature Astrid appreciated, would be a great help too, once the bairn came.

For the rest, Astrid still tended her mother's Winter Garden, a lovely scheduled walled garden on the top level of the keep, and spent time with Mairi in the afternoons in the ladies' solar.

As her belly had grown over the past moons, she'd ceased practicing with her knives or going out on long rides with Finn—both activities brought her much joy, yet she was wary of falling from her horse, and her big belly affected her balance when knife-throwing.

"Finn's out there, isn't he?"

Mairi's voice roused her, and Astrid cut her a glance to find her sister-by-marriage smiling.

"How did ye know?" she asked, arching a brow.

Mairi inclined her head, her gaze glinting. "Ye get a glow to yer face whenever ye look his way."

Astrid gave a soft, embarrassed laugh before waving to her husband.

With a wink, Finn walked off.

Rubbing her lower back, which had been paining her ever since she'd risen from her bed that morning, Astrid leaned against the stone window ledge. "Ye get a similar expression upon yer face whenever ye look Loch's way," she pointed out.

Mairi laughed. "Aye ... I'm more in love with him now than I ever was." She shook her head then. "I didn't think it was possible."

"Aye, the love that develops when ye spend time with someone is magical indeed," she mused. "It's different from how things are at the beginning ... when everything is stomach-churning and exciting. When true affection grows between ye, it's as if the pair of ye grow roots ... and those roots knit together."

Mairi smiled back. "That's exactly how it feels."

Astrid pushed herself off the window ledge then, heading back toward the chair. She and Mairi were busy sewing clothing for the coming bairn, and she was halfway through a wee shift that would be perfect for the warmer months.

However, she'd only taken two steps when a strange sensation fluttered through her lower belly. An instant later, liquid cascaded between her thighs.

Gasping, Astrid halted, her hand grasping her stomach.

"Astrid?" Mairi's eyes flew wide. Rising to her feet, she set Greig down on the mat before the unlit hearth. "Are ye in pain?"

Astrid watched liquid pool upon the wooden floor under her skirts, her breath catching. "No ... but I think the bairn is on its way."

Astrid surprised everyone at Duart, the midwife included, by giving birth quickly. Once the birthing pains arrived, a short while after her waters broke, they seized her with vicious intent. Teeth gritted, she bore down with each pain as Flora, the midwife, instructed. And then, a little before midnight, the bairn was born.

The lass barely uttered a squeak, making nothing more than a tiny mewling sound when Flora wrapped her up in a soft woolen shawl and passed her to Astrid.

Still panting from that last push, her body slick with sweat and aching, Astrid grinned.

She didn't care that she'd weathered agony over the past hours.

The sight of this perfect tiny creature, cradled in her arms, made everything worth it.

"Can I come in?" The door to the birthing chamber had opened a crack, and Finn peeked inside. His face was pale and strained, and Astrid knew without having to ask that he'd have worn a groove in the wooden boards outside the chamber as he waited for her to give birth.

He'd wanted to be at her side while she labored, yet Flora had ushered him out, telling him that men brought bad luck at births. Astrid had been disappointed, for she'd wanted Finn there. Nonetheless, she knew folk could be superstitious about such things, and Flora wasn't a woman to be argued with.

The midwife's facial expression was much softer now as she beckoned to Finn. "Aye, lad … come see yer bonnie daughter."

Delight flowered across Finn's face, and he moved forward, covering the distance to Astrid's side in just a couple of strides. Sinking down onto the stool next to her, he leaned in, his lips brushing her sweaty brow. "Ye have done well, my love." His gaze then dropped to his daughter's scrunched-up red face. "She's beautiful, indeed."

"She's ours, Finn," Astrid replied huskily. "Look what our love has made."

Finn's breathing hitched, and a moment later, tears sparkled upon his lashes.

"She was certainly impatient to arrive," Flora piped up. "I've birthed few bairns who've come so quickly."

"It didn't feel fast to me," Finn muttered. "Each hour I waited outside that door was an eternity."

"Aye, well … trust me, lad … many a husband has waited a day or two to see his bairn."

Astrid's mouth grimaced at this. She was relieved the labor hadn't been drawn out, and that despite her narrow hips, the babe hadn't gotten stuck.

"We haven't discussed names," she told Finn, breaking eye contact then to look at her daughter's face. "What should we call her?"

Moments passed, and when Finn didn't answer, Astrid glanced up. His face was solemn now, his eyes still gleaming with emotion. "How about 'Maggie'?"

Astrid stared back at him, surprised.

Aye, over the past year, they'd sometimes spoken of her friend. They'd even visited her grave together. It had been overgrown with weeds, as if her family had now forgotten about her, and so Astrid and Finn had tidied it up and placed a bouquet of wildflowers before the small wooden cross that was beginning to rot. A few weeks later, Finn had replaced the cross with one made of stone—one that would last.

It was a lovely gesture, one which Astrid had appreciated. The local fisherfolk had learned of what Finn had done too, although many of them remained suspicious of him all the same.

Sometimes, Astrid was tempted to go to them, to tell them the truth, yet she always hesitated. Maggie was gone, and bringing up the tragedy again would only dredge up past hurts. Her father had declared Finn innocent, and the folk of Craignure would have to grow to accept it.

Nonetheless, there was sometimes a reserve between them if Maggie ever came up in conversation, almost as if her ghost hadn't been laid completely to rest.

"Are ye sure?" Astrid asked after a pause.

He nodded. "If *ye* are." His voice roughened. "It feels ... right ... somehow."

Astrid smiled, even as her throat tightened and her vision misted. She thought then of her spirited yet fey friend who'd craved the love and attention she'd never received at home, and whose life had been tragically cut short. There was a part of Astrid that felt as if she'd failed her, and when she'd told Finn that, he admitted he felt the same way.

They'd all been young and self-absorbed in those days, barely able to see past their own noses. Neither of them had understood how fragile Maggie was.

In truth, Astrid had been tempted to give the bairn her mother's name, Gellise, yet Finn's suggestion stuck with her. "Very well then," she said softly, her fingers tracing the bairn's cheek. "Greetings, Maggie MacDonald."

The End

HISTORICAL NOTES

In this novel, we take a trip from the Isle of Mull to the Isle of Skye.

If you've read my BRIDES OF SKYE series, you will have already visited Dunvegan Castle and met Malcolm Macleod … a few decades in the future.

THE LADY HE LOATHED takes place in 1315 while THE BEAST'S BRIDE (BOOK #1: THE BRIDES OF SKYE) starts in 1346. Malcolm Macleod is nineteen in our tale and took over from his father, Tormod, as clan-chief in 1320 when he was 24. And I've kept his brash character in keeping with the man he later becomes.

Dunvegan Castle is a beautifully preserved fortress on the northwestern edge of the Isle of Skye and is still owned by the Macleods. Likely a fortified site from ancient times, the castle was first built in the 13th century and developed bit by bit over the centuries. In the 19th century, the whole castle was remodeled in a mock-medieval style. It's built on an elevated rock overlooking an inlet on the eastern shore of Loch Dunvegan, a sea loch.

Duart Castle and Dounarwyse Castle both feature in this novel too. Duart dates back to the 13th Century and is the seat of clan Maclean, whereas Dounarwyse (known today as Aros Castle) is a ruined 13th-century castle near Salen, overlooking the Sound of Mull.

There were a couple of Scottish slang/terms or Scottish Gaelic words that appear in this novel, that may need elaborating on:

Spoots: razor clams—shellfish with a long, tubular shell. There are a few local methods of 'hunting' spoots. Find out more here: https://gallowaywildfoods.com/march-spoot-clamsrazor-clams/

Spùinneadair-mara (spoo-nuder mara): in Gaelic this means plunderer, spoiler, or robber on the sea. Or more specifically, a pirate.

Although I didn't base the Siege of Dounarwyse on an actual battle, the clan conflicts that take place in this series are based on real feuds between the Macleans of Duart and the Mackinnons of Dùn Ara. Traditionally, the Macleans of Duart were allies of the Macleods of Skye, and the Mackinnons of Dùn Ara were allied to the MacDonalds of Sleat on the Isle of Skye. It's always fun, and far more authentic, to anchor my stories on real history!

As always, I hope these notes give you an insight into the research I do, and into the rich culture and history my novels anchor themselves on.

DIVE INTO MY BACKLIST!

Check out my printable reading order list on my website: https://www.jaynecastel.com/printable-reading-list

ABOUT THE AUTHOR

Multi-award-winning author Jayne Castel writes epic Historical and Fantasy Romance. Her vibrant characters, richly researched historical settings, and action-packed adventure romance transport readers to forgotten times and imaginary worlds.

Jayne is the author of a number of best-selling series. A hopeless romantic in love with all things Scottish, she writes romances set in both Dark Ages and Medieval Scotland, and Romantasy with a Celtic vibe.

When she's not writing, Jayne is reading (and re-reading) her favorite authors, cooking Italian feasts, and going on long walks with her husband. She's from New Zealand but now lives in Edinburgh, Scotland.

Connect with Jayne online:
www.jaynecastel.com
www.facebook.com/JayneCastelRomance
https://www.instagram.com/jaynecastelauthor/
Email: **contact@jaynecastel.com**